The Three Lives of Kamala

Timothy J. Lomperis

Hidden Mentor Media

PRAISE FOR THE THREE LIVES OF KAMALA

by Nanda Rao

This book is a heartwarming read of Indian mythology intertwined with creative fictional storytelling, beautifully woven together from the point of view of the author's perspective from spending several years in India during his childhood.

~Ms. Nanda Rao, a film producer who divides her time between Hollywood and Bollywood

CONTENTS

Map of Ancient India

PROLOGUE

J ust as in the West, classical India has a rich history of stories. But the path of these stories can be different because the beliefs in these two cultures are not always the same. In the West, for example, people live one life, and then go on to their reward (or punishment). In classical Hindu India, however, people can go through several lives before they attain their reward, or moksha (which, instead of salvation, means "release" from having to be reborn). This is one such story.

India is a large triangular peninsula, about one-third the size of the United States that juts into the Indian Ocean from Central Asia. It is walled off from this vast continent by a rooftop of mountains that are the highest in the *world: the Himalayas. The Grandest of them, mythically, is Mount Meru. Like Mount Olympus in Greece, it is the dwelling of the gods. From these mountains, and their melting snows, flow India's many rivers, including the sacred Ganges, and its purifying waters. On this river lies the ancient city of Vijayapura, where this story takes place. It is set at the close of the late medieval period (thirteenth to sixteenth centuries) of Indian history. Vijayapura is the fictional capital city of a Rajput kingdom of North India. Golconda is one of the Muslim sultanates of the Deccan Plateau of South India—famous for its diamonds.*

Hindu Indian tradition is grounded in the belief that the dancing god of the cosmos, Lord Shiva, holds together the life rhythm of mountains, rivers, animals, and people. Vijayapura is home to the attractive widow, Kamala, and her son, Raju. What unfolds is the story of the eternal love between mother and child, who were tragically separated, as they strive to be reunited across many places and many lives.

Introduction: Lord Shiva's Worry

Lord Shiva sat on his throne on Mount Meru, the Olympian home of the Hindu gods of India. As he looked down on the huge Indo-Gangetic plain, the sacred rivers, and teeming cities, he leaned over to his wife, the goddess Parvati. He was worried. "I am beginning to see dangers growing for a terrible war in India."

"When you see things like this, you always have a plan," Parvati said.

"We could make this right ourselves. After all, we are gods," Lord Shiva observed.

"But..." Parvati smiled. "I know what's coming."

"Humans have to make their own destinies. They must learn to turn to their higher natures and pray to us for guidance. Then we can point them to a proper path," Lord Shiva explained.

"This time, my Lord, let a woman lead the way."

"Yes, yes. There will be a woman, and her son. But let's start with two swans."

CHAPTER 1

THE KING AND THE WHITE SWAN

On the ground, in Medieval India, all was not well. This was odd. India was prosperous and at peace. Its rivers watered the plains that provided life for crops, animals, and people. Most sacred of these rivers was the Ganges. Its flowing waters offered purifying baths for the sins of the living and currents to dissolve the ashes of the dead.

Another great river, the Yamuna, flowed into the Ganges.

Where these rivers met sat the capital of a Rajput Kingdom that reigned over most of North India. In fact, its ruler, King Chandra Gupta, had just defeated Golconda, a Muslim kingdom in South India. To commemorate his triumph, he re-named the capital Victory City, or Vijayapura. But the victory brought him more worry than peace.

In the middle of Vijayapura rose the walls and towers of King Chandra Gupta's palace with its gardens, pools, fountains, flowers—and pond. It was all luxury, yet in the very halls and alcoves of the palace, plots, conspiracies, and treacheries swirled like invisible serpents hissing their poisonous venom. Or so Chandra Gupta imagined.

On this day, the king, who was in his early forties, lounged uneasily on a couch in the royal gardens while being entertained by the ladies of the court. One of them cooled the king's forehead with a fan of peacock feathers. Another tickled the king's chin to get him to laugh. Even from afar, the colors the king wore were striking—his bright red velvet vest, shiny white pants, and gold pointed toe slippers flaunted his power. What stood out, however, was his silk crimson turban. In the middle perched a huge diamond glinting rays of silver, steel blue, and blazing gold all at once. Everywhere the king went, eyes were drawn to this diamond, like a whirlpool pulling in its prey. The diamond symbolized King Chandra Gupta's wealth and power, and he wore it all the time.

It was a "gift" from the *Nawab* of Golconda, Haider Ali. Golconda was in South India, and the people of this kingdom followed a different religion, Islam, and normally kept apart from the Hindu lands in the north that worshipped Lord Shiva. But Chandra Gupta wanted to expand his power over South India. So, he had marched to the border of Golconda with his terrifying armed elephants. Haider Ali tried to storm Chandra Gupta's army with his fine cavalry of Arabian horses, but the horses panicked when the elephants reared on their hind legs, lifted their trunks, and shattered the sky with their screeching trumpets. Haider Ali surrendered into a forced alliance and gave Chandra Gupta the diamond as a token of submission and loyalty to the Rajput Kingdom.

But today King Chandra Gupta was distracted. He was angry and confused because he had received reports that Haider Ali grumbled about his forced alliance with Vijayapura. In fact, Chandra Gupta's advisors warned him there were spies from Golconda—in his own court—plotting for the return of the diamond.

Whenever the king was frustrated like this, he sought refuge in the royal pond (really a small lake). It was a special pond, even a divine pond. It was called the Lotus Pond. There were lotus pads with beautiful white lotus flowers that ringed the pond. The lotus was the flower of India and was the symbol of the Hindu belief in *samsara*, the divine path to *moksha*, the relief of the soul to heaven, through the path of reincarnation through many lives. Indeed, the water of this royal pond was rumored to be from the divine waters of forgetfulness from Heaven that transported new souls to their next reincarnation.

Chandra Gupta's worries right now, however, were more political than spiritual. He climbed into a boat and rowed out to the middle of the Lotus Pond to think. Soon the king's favorite swan, Rani, swam alongside the boat with her little male swan cygnet, Babu, on her back. Rani was the king's favorite of all the palace creatures. She, and a shimmering black male swan, Raja, were gifts to Chandra Gupta from the distant king of Persia. Rani had a black beak with an unusual vivid orange tip.

"Good day to you, Rani. How is my queen today? And how is Babu? Is your little boy behaving?" These questions were always the ritual that began their visits.

Rani understood the king's need to vent. She always listened intently to everything the king said, and he used the swan as his sounding board for his plans and reflections. He often spent hours with the swan in the middle of the pond.

"Rani, I had to get away from those women. I cannot think with all their fussing. You need to listen to me. I've got a lot on my mind."

Rani nodded.

"First of all, now that I have conquered all these lands, even Golconda in the South, how can I keep them? I need an heir so my family can rule Vijayapura far into the future. You have your little Babu; who, I am sure, will follow you everywhere—even through many lives of *samsara*. But I do not have my cygnet, just my baby daughter, Lakshmi, and she cannot inherit the throne. Her mother died in childbirth. Unless I marry again and produce an heir, I am doomed to die without an heir to carry on my legacy.

Rani shot a quizzical look at the king as Babu jumped off her back and swam around her in circles. Mother swan and cygnet son had a tight bond. Most swan families are distant and aloof—father from mother, parent from child. They glide through the water like strangers. Not this pair. Babu spent his days circling playfully around his mother. She, in turn, would tease him by pushing him under the water with her orange beak. He loved to dive deep into the water and surprise his mother by bursting up to the surface behind her tail feathers or just under her long neck. Then Rani would always act surprised and splash him with her wings. It was a game that could occupy half the day. The king loved to watch these antics.

Still, there was a sadness that hung over the pair because their circle of love was not complete. The jet-black swan, Raja, life-long mate of Rani and father of the cygnet, was seldom with them in the royal pond. While Rani and Babu came to love the royal pond and their "conversations" with King Chandra Gupta, Raja yearned for the cool rivers and clear lakes of their native Persia.

To reach Persia, Raja had to fly over the roof top of the world, the mighty Himalaya Mountains. His flight path took him frequently by Mount Meru. The noble black swan was a pleasing sight to the gods on the mountain. Raja came to know these mountains well with their rich forests, steep cliffs, glaciers, and hidden caves. Indeed, Lord Shiva once asked him to be the divine swan of the sacred mountain. Raja declined because on his return flights from Persia, he longed to be reunited with his family on the royal lake in Vijayapura.

Nevertheless, one day Lord Shiva stopped Raja long enough to give him a gift.

"Stop, Raja. Stop," thundered Lord Shiva. "With all your flying about, I need to give you a mission."

Raja lit down on the arm of Lord Shiva's throne. "What is it you want me to do, my Lord?"

"You have become part of a plan I have for the *moksha* (salvation) of a family that is dear to me. If the plan fails, there may be a terrible war. Much of this plan depends on you. Stay here close to me because at just a certain moment you must fly to the great Himalayan waterfall and help a man who will fall from this waterfall. Between you and this man there will be a bond. I am giving you the gift of human speech with him, just as he will be given the gift of bird speech with you.

Meanwhile, at the Lotus Pond, King Chandra Gupta had become agitated. "And, speaking of Golconda, despite this diamond in my turban, I don't trust Haider Ali. I know he has spies here in the palace. He has sons, so his future in *his* kingdom is secure. Who knows what these spies are up to? What plot is Haider Ali hatching?"

As usual, Chandra Gupta's imagination got the better of him. When this happened, Rani always shook her beak, and the king would stop. Not this time. Babu stopped swimming. The two swans, mother and son, gaped at the king. With an exclamation of "Traitor!" Chandra Gupta turned sharply, and, stabbing the water with his oars, he churned the boat back to the shore. He got out of the boat and stomped through the gardens into the palace. He told an aide to summon Indra Singh, the Commander of the Palace Guard.

CHAPTER 2

THE LOST DIAMOND

When the king turned the boat around, Rani flapped her wings to get out of the way. In all this thrashing, she was alert enough to hear a distinctive plop and see a glittering object plummeting down to the bottom of the pond. Forgetting Babu, she dove in pursuit. As always, her trusting cygnet followed. At the bottom, Rani's beak nudged up this most brilliant of all stones.

She eagerly put it into her mouth. But she was so excited she accidentally swallowed it. With all her panicked thrashing to cough out this huge stone from her slender throat, she unintentionally crushed Babu, who had followed too closely. In this terrifying and needless way, choking and crushing, the lives of the two swans came to an end.

Meanwhile, the king commanded Indra Singh to announce an assembly of all his vassal kings, or *rajas*, to consider the rumors that had so upset him. Called *Durbars*, they were summoned by grand kings or emperors to take up urgent matters of state. Sometimes *Durbars* were called by the king to ask for advice on some problem that was vexing him. At other times the king summoned his *rajas* to announce and explain new laws. More often they were ordered to proclaim changes to his government and introduce new appointments. Then there were the rare occasions when a *Durbar* was called to demand loyalty in the face of a suspected conspiracy. This was one of those occasions: to expose the conspiracy that the king was sure was coming from the *Nawab* of Golconda, Haider Ali. To emphasize its severity, he dressed all in gray, and even left his turban back in his quarters.

Chandra Gupta began. "I see you are all in your places, except for Haider Ali." He then turned to Haider Ali's ambassador. "And where, do tell, is Haider Ali? It is a solemn oath sworn by all my *rajas* that when I call a *Durbar,* all must attend."

The ambassador shifted uncomfortably in his seat. "He is back in Golconda attending the royal wedding of his son, and heir, your Majesty."

"Why was I not invited to give my blessings to this marriage?" the king demanded.

The ambassador hesitated. "Your Majesty, my lord thought that he should conduct the wedding more privately so you would not feel obligated to make such a long journey to the South in this hot season." He waited before adding, slyly, "Haider Ali also did not want to give offense because of your own—'situation.'"

The king rose from his throne and thundered, "My own situation!" After a time, he sat back down realizing he was revealing too much unease over not having a son. In a calmer voice, he turned to the ambassador. "Tell Haider Ali that I expect him back in court so I can present him with a gift celebrating the marriage of his son. This is how I will show my continued commitment to the peace treaty that ended your ruler's little rebellion from my offer of an alliance, which, at first, he dared to refuse." He paused, and then warned the ambassador. "If a secret journey to Golconda for a private wedding has caught Haider Ali unable to attend a *Durbar*, it does not remove him from suspicion to the rumors I hear around court that he is plotting to overthrow me."

"I can assure you—" the ambassador began.

Chandra Gupta cut him off. "I will take assurances only from Haider Ali face-to-face."

The king then turned to the others. "What about all of you? Is there any truth to these rumors? Are any of you up to things I should know about? It would be better to tell me now so that I do not have to find out the hard way. And, if we find out there is something going on, can I count on your loyalty to Vijayapura?"

One by one all at the *Durbar* professed, "You can count on my loyalty, your Highness."

After the last one spoke, the king sat motionless in an uncomfortably long pause before uttering a tentative "Good." Clearly not convinced, Chandra Gupta rose, concluding the *Durbar*. The *Rajas* filed out of the chamber, quiet and anxious. They knew a cloud of suspicion hung over all of them.

After the *Durbar,* the king ordered Indra Singh to retrieve his turban he had left behind in his private quarters. In fetching it, Indra Singh noticed the Golconda diamond was missing from the king's turban. This, he knew, was a grave crisis.

The king, of course, was furious. "What are you saying? How can it be just missing?" Chandra Gupta demanded. "Someone stole it during the *Durbar.* Haider Ali, I am sure, is responsible."

"Your Highness, we do not know that. You cannot go accusing anyone without absolute proof. You'll trigger a civil war with the first false accusation." Indra Singh then tried to calm the king. "Your Highness, I will have a fake diamond made to put in your turban that will shine just as brightly as the real one. No one else must know the diamond is missing. If they do, most will assume Haider Ali is the culprit. But there are those who might conspire to frame him so that you will attack Haider Ali by mistake, perhaps get killed yourself, and leave the path to the kingship open to conspirators. No, we must be absolutely certain of who stole it, or discover conclusively that it is simply lost. I make you this solemn vow: if the diamond has just been lost, I will not show my face again in your court until I find it, because the security of the diamond in your custody is my responsibility. So, you can relax knowing at least that, while I am away, none of your *rajas* is yet guilty."

Chandra Gupta waved his hand. "And if you do find the diamond, which you seem to think is unlikely?"

Indra Singh was appalled at the king's thinking. "Your Majesty, this is my sacred promise that I make before you and our god, Lord Shiva: you shall not see me again without the Golconda Diamond in my hand. If I fail in my search, you must kill me for betraying my trust to safeguard the diamond, rather than blindly accuse one of your *rajas*, and start another war. When you see me again at court, I will either not have the diamond in my hand, and deserve death, or hold it in my hand with a full account of how it was lost—and found."

The king turned white. "Why such a deadly vow, Indra Singh?

Indra Singh frowned and drew close to the king. "Your Majesty, you need to let the Rajas and Haider Ali know that I am on a secret mission. This will put them all on edge. If one of them stole the diamond, he will become flustered and exhibit behaviors that will arouse the suspicions of my friends at court. They will look out for the conspirator's next move, which will likely be to sneak the stolen diamond away from the court and conceal it on his estate—where I will catch him. In the meantime, my Lord, conduct your business as if nothing were wrong. If you stay calm, Vijayapura will stay calm."

Chandra Gupta was still worried. "Besides Rani, the swan, I have come to rely on you for kingly advice. I don't know if I can manage without your steady hand."

"Your Majesty, we all rely on Bikshu, the Palace Priest, for spiritual guidance. Take him now into greater confidence. More than I, he can align the destiny of your reign with the cosmic plans of Lord Shiva."

With this deadly oath of loyalty, Indra Singh set out from the palace on his quest, warning that it might take years to accomplish his mission. Nevertheless, with Indra Singh's selfless vow to solve the mystery of the diamond's disappearance, Chandra Gupta felt strangely at ease.

In all this commotion, except for the royal gardener, no one noticed the beautiful swan and tiny cygnet floating, lifeless, on the Lotus Pond. Not wanting to upset the king any further, the doting gardener took the favored bird and her drowned offspring to the Palace Priest, Bikshu. Bikshu honored the two birds with a special cremation ceremony on the banks of the sacred River Ganges. As he lit their funeral pyres, he prayed. "Now my noble swans, may you fulfill the destiny that Lord Shiva desires for all the souls that will follow from you."

The gardener was surprised. "The swans are dead, Bikshu."

The priest replied. "Their souls are not."

Bikshu had been the Palace Priest for a long time. No one knew for how long. He seemed timeless. The harmony of Lord Shiva's dance radiated a peace from his eyes. In fact, his spiritual gifts from Lord Shiva gave him a deep knowledge of the past —and, sometimes, foreknowledge of the future.

Thus challenged by the gardener, Bikshu explained, "My good and faithful gardener, we Hindus believe people undergo reincarnations—or rebirths—of many lives before they can escape to the salvation that is a release from Lord Shiva's dance. This is called *moksha*."

"I don't understand a word you're saying," replied the very confused gardener.

"Let me try a different approach, then," Bikshu replied. "I have a special gift from Lord Shiva. I can remember the path of my own cycle of lives—past, present, and even hints about my future—and of those whose lives join with mine. I can see beyond the heavenly River of Forgetfulness that washes out the remembrance of previous lives for most people when they die. Because of this gift, the king, and members of the royal court consult me on how they can be faithful to Lord Shiva's plan for their life cycles. Would you like me to help you with yours?"

"No!" replied the horrified gardener. "I wouldn't understand, and I don't want to know anything about the future. The present is enough of a bother."

Bikshu sighed. "Your path to *moksha* and remembrance, my dear gardener, will be long.

After the ceremony, Bikshu went to tell the king about the loss of the swan and her baby cygnet. He used the occasion to foretell King Chandra Gupta his destiny. "Your majesty, the loss of these two swans will trigger a series of lives that will lead to three main events in your life: the quest for something lost, your release from the cares of this world; and, along the way, the furnishing of heirs to the throne of Vijayapura."

Chandra Gupta looked at Bikshu, puzzled. He thought to himself: *"Thanks to Indra Singh, I can believe in the return of the diamond, and maybe even moksha, but heirs?"*

Bikshu cut in on his thoughts. "I know what you're thinking, your Majesty; yes, heirs.

It was not long before a threat to the secret of the diamond rose in the person of Raman Pandu. Raman Pandu served as one of the captains of the Palace Guard under the commander, Indra Singh. As a captain, Raman was known for having very sharp eyes, which he used on more than one occasion to save King Chandra Gupta's life. But it was these sharp eyes that brought about his disgrace. One day, he looked a little too sharply at the king's turban and told the king that he noticed that the diamond in his turban was a fake. He expected to be rewarded for this observation.

Instead, the king demanded harshly, "And how do you know this?"

"Your highness, my wife, Kamala, wears a diamond necklace all the time. It was given to her by her mother, Parvati. A true diamond shines with many colors, but the strongest is always blue. The light from the stone in your turban is only white," Raman explained.

Chandra Gupta now remembered that Indra Singh's wife, Parvati, was from a priestly family, known as Brahmins, the highest social class *caste* in

India. Parvati was the name of the goddess wife of Lord Shiva, and this human Parvati seemed to many who knew her to be a goddess herself. This is why Chandra Gupta had appointed Indra Singh the commander of the Palace Guard in the first place. He needed the loyal support of Vijayapura's leading families. But now Chandra Gupta needed to get rid of Raman Pandu—for fear the secret of the missing diamond would break out. Raman had committed the unpardonable sin in any kingly court: he knew too much.

The next day Raman was summoned to a private audience with the king. "Captain Pandu, you are mistaken about my diamond. It is absolutely genuine. You must not share this crazy idea of yours with anyone! Do I make myself absolutely clear?"

Again, taken aback, Raman nodded. "Of course, your majesty."

But the king did not like the questioning look on Raman's face. He needed to get him out of the court, fast. "Captain Pandu," the king said, "I have a special mission for you in honor of all the service your sharp eyes have given me. You are to take your company of guards to capture Afghan raiders who are plundering the people of the Himalaya Mountains. If you are successful, you must then try to discover the whereabouts or fate of your commander, Indra Singh, before returning to court."

It was a suicide mission. The mere 200 men in Raman's company were no match for the estimated 1,000 Afghan raiders. Soon rumors circulated that Raman and his men had all been killed. Back home in Vijayapura, Chandra Gupta became afraid Raman Pandu might have shared his misgivings about the king's diamond with Kamala, or even might hear from Raman Pandu, if he were somehow still alive. As a precaution, he banished

Kamala from the court. However, he let her come to the temple whenever she liked. Chandra Gupta knew Kamala was a devout woman. Besides, Bikshu was at the temple, and could keep track of Kamala's doings. Meanwhile, Kamala told Raju his father was dead, and she was a widow. However, as a token of the fine family she came from, even in exile, she wore her diamond necklace every day.

CHAPTER 3

KABADDI

Ten years had passed since Indra Singh left on his quest for the missing diamond—and since Raman Pandu disappeared. Because neither could show his face at court, to the people of Vijayapura rather than real persons they became legends. King Chandra Gupta tried to move on to other concerns of the realm. He wore a cleverly fake diamond in his turban, but the secret loss of the real diamond weighed him down—and he doubted that Bikshu's prophecy of heirs would come true.

As the royal priest of the palace temple, Bikshu ran a school for the children of the court. He also insisted that the poor children who lived around the palace attend the school as well. This meant that children from all the social castes and classes could come. Among these children were Raju, the son of Kamala and the grandson of Indra Singh, and Lakshmi, the daughter of the king. They were both ten years old and were drawn to each other. But they were too shy, and nervous, to admit it—so they teased each other mercilessly.

Rumors of palace intrigue and plots among the *Rajas* at court swirled around the palace, and even flowed around the temple school, but the knowledge of the missing diamond did not swim in any of these currents. The way Bikshu hovered around Raju and Lakshmi, however, was beginning to attract the attention of the other students. Bikshu could not avoid this because he knew that the dance of the Lord Shiva swirled close to this young pair.

One day, after kidding back and forth, Lakshmi stretched her neck to take out a sudden kink. Raju noticed and blurted, "I don't care what you think about your ugly this and that, you are as beautiful as a swan."

Lakshmi was taken aback. She blushed. "Why a swan?"

"Your neck curves so gracefully."

"But swans have such long necks. I would be ugly with a swan's neck. I am named after Lakshmi, the goddess of beauty, after all."

It was afternoon after school, and the two wandered towards the far end of the Lotus Pond to feed the new palace swans. Lakshmi sidled up to Raju as one of the swans pecked at the bread in her outstretched hand. She turned to Raju. "Why do you always come by the swans every day? Were you a swan in a previous life?"

"Sometimes, I think I was," mused Raju. "Aren't they just the most beautiful things?"

Lakshmi blushed, remembering that he had just called her a swan. "Well, if you think I'm a swan, too; maybe as a girl I need something around my neck, so my bare neck wouldn't look so long."

Raju looked at her, and quietly said, "Maybe you do." With that, he turned abruptly away from the pond.

"Where are you going?" she asked, running to catch up.

"Off to play *kabaddi* before going home to supper with Mother."

"Mind if I tag along?"

"Who's stopping you?"

As they walked toward the *kabaddi* court, Lakshmi vented. "You know, you are lucky to have a mother. My mother died giving birth to me. Now Father just has me, and I feel he is disappointed because I'm a girl and cannot become king."

Raju stopped and looked at her. "I am not disappointed that you're a girl. Besides, who says you can't be king?"

"You really are crazy, you know that." She changed the subject. "You and your mother are very close, aren't you?"

"Yes, we are," said Raju, "like a swan and her cygnet."

The pair walked to the *kabaddi* court. Already a dozen children had lined up on the two sides of the court. It had two parallel lines about 50 feet apart. The game started with an even number of players behind each line forming the two teams. When a player crossed his line, he had to shout "*kabaddi, kabaddi, kabaddi*" until he ran out of breath, at which point he had to run back across his line. Naturally, players behind the opposite line did the same thing. Hence, it was when the opposing players met in the middle that the drama of the game began. Players from the two teams would hold onto their opponents until players ran out of breath and could no longer shout "*kabaddi.*" The out-of-breath player was then captured and taken to "prison" along the opposing team's line. If one of his teammates could tag him while still shouting "*kabaddi, kabaddi, kabaddi,*" the prisoner was set free, and could return to his line. The game was over when one side captured all the players from the opposing team.

The game was fast-moving and required a mix of skills among the players: strong, heavy ones who could hold opponents tight, ones with long breaths who could break free, and fast, wiggly ones. It also took strategy: quick players to dash out first and capture unsuspecting opponents, followed by the heavy players to hold the captives fast, and, on the other side, wiggly ones with long breaths who could break free from the heavy players, and even move on to free prisoners before running out of breath. Since it was hard to tell just when a player had run out of breath and was trying to sneak by a *kabaddi* or two on a secret second breath, there had to be an umpire to catch this. If the game was "serious," Bikshu was always the umpire.

In these duties he had a helper. Always hovering over the game was Vijaya, Bikshu's magpie. Like parrots, magpies can imitate human speech, and even converse. Vijaya looked like the common crow, except he was a little bigger and proudly sported white wing feathers that stood out from the jet-black feathers on the rest of his body. His main job was to carry messages back and forth from the heavenly Mount Meru to Bikshu's temple, and to go on scouting missions around the kingdom of Vijayapura. But what Vijaya loved to do most was to serve as the final referee on whether a *kabaddi* player had drawn a second breath. If he spied a cheater on a second breath, he would screech "*Kabaddi!*" and peck the ears of the offender. What he liked most about these games, however, was that he could play with Raju and Lakshmi, his favorites.

With so many players already lined up on both sides, this was to be a serious game. Raju and Lakshmi were always a pair in serious games. Raju drew in an almost supernaturally long breath, and he was so wiggly he was impossible to hold. Lakshmi would dart back and forth along her line so opponents could not track her, and then burst from the line with the speed of a tigress to either free a teammate or capture an opponent.

After a half hour of running and struggling, the game neared its close. Both sides were panting with exhaustion. Following an enormous struggle, Raju brought in two opposing players to "prison." Only one player on the opposing team remained. With a last burst of energy, Raju charged after him, grabbed him, and started pulling him back to Raju's line. But Raju had run out too fast and was losing his breath. This threatened to turn the tables with the other player capturing Raju instead with his fresher breath. Vijaya circled over Raju, but just as he was about to give out, Lakshmi dashed in, freshly screaming "*kabaddi, kabaddi, kabaddi*" and pulled the player that Raju was still holding over their line as the player's breath collapsed. Vijaya flew off. The game was over.

Breathlessly, Lakshmi danced up to the wheezing Raju. "This swan just rescued you."

Raju just smiled.

As the players dispersed, Bikshu approached the pair. "Great move, Lakshmi. And, Raju, you are always the steady one. Children, Lord Shiva's dance plays on through the rounds of our many lives; and, in his dance, your destinies are intertwined."

"How?" they both asked.

"It is not for me to say now," Bikshu said. "But Lakshmi will know when she finds Raju's mother in another few rounds of Lord Shiva's dance."

"What?" they both asked again. Then they looked at each other—and blushed.

Disheveled, exhausted, but very pleased with the intriguing moments of the afternoon, Raju finally arrived home—to his very preoccupied mother, Kamala.

CHAPTER 4

KAMALA

Kamala was an attractive woman in her thirties who lived with her son Raju in a modest home near the palace. Her husband, Captain Raman Pandu, had served in the Palace Guard, so the home was sturdy. There were three rooms with mud plaster walls, a wooden door, a packed, smoothed dirt floor, and a thick thatched roof. In the back there was a small yard where Kamala kept two cows, a goat, and a few egg-laying hens.

Despite her modest home, Kamala came from a good family. Her father, none other than Indra

Singh, the missing commander of the Palace Guard, was from India's elite warrior class or caste. It was now ten years since he left Vijayapura on his secret quest, and Raju had never met his legendary grandfather. Indeed, Raju also had no memory of his father, Raman Pandu, for he had left the palace in disgrace, and had been reported as missing.

As a token of her loyalty to her missing husband, every day Kamala wore the diamond necklace he had given her at their wedding. As beautiful as the necklace was, the orange mole under Kamala's right eye is what drew people to her—its color was the same as her twin originated name, Kamala from the South which meant "orange," and Kamala the lotus flower, a symbol of samsara. Everyone thought it was a divine sign. The origins of this mole went back to the time ten years ago when Indra Singh's and Raman Pandu's departed from the court—and when the swans had died and the diamond had disappeared, and Indra Singh was sent off on his secret mission to find it.

At that time Kamala was very pregnant. The palace temple served as something of a hospital, and there was a midwife at the temple to help the women give birth to their babies. Kamala's time came, and she hurried to the temple, where the midwife had a special room waiting. Soon she gave birth to a healthy, screaming boy. But then she began to choke and gag. The midwife could do nothing to help Kamala. She ran to Bikshu because she thought Kamala was dying and needed the priest's blessing for her journey to the afterlife.

Bikshu came running, and shouted, "Everyone out. I need to be with Kamala alone." They all left but heard Bikshu reciting *mantras* over Kamala's thrashing body. The thrashing ceased, and Kamala returned to the world of the living as if she had just been dead. Bikshu then allowed the midwife back in to bathe the baby.

The father and husband, Raman Pandu, also came in and held the boy, and said, "Let us call the child, Raju, my son with the special destiny." At this joyous moment, Raman hardly realized that he would not see his son for another ten years.

There was something else he noticed, and he said, "Kamala, my sweet, I see you have a new orange mole under your right eye. It must be a mark of insight from the goddess, Parvati."

Kamala was still retching and rubbing an itch under her right eye. "So that's what it is," she exclaimed. "I don't know why I should be coughing and scratching during childbirth."

"It is strange," Raman conceded. "You are always inquiring about the journey of your soul. Somehow, I am sure the coughing, the mole, and especially our precious little son will help you find your way." The mark, or mole, that appeared with the birth of Raju would stay with Kamala for the rest of her soul's journey. In the death of the two swans and Raju's birth, the souls of the swans and human mother and infant had become intertwined. But they had forgotten how.

Remembered or not, it had been a rough passage. Two things were going on at once— separately at first. Rani, the swan, was diving after the diamond with Babu too close behind. Meanwhile, Kamala was undergoing the pangs of childbirth. Somehow, underneath the Lotus Pond divine waters from the Heavenly River of Forgetfulness opened up transporting the pair of thrashing, dying swans into Bhikshu's nearby birthing room in the temple. From these waters, Rani and Babu melted into Kamala and her baby in ways that cannot be humanly described. The thrashing of the swans now shook Kamala's body. The waters receded taking the dead swans back to the lake, while Kamala gave birth to Raju with the orange mole erupting under her eye. It, indeed, had been a strange birth. But all was forgotten—except for the mole.

That was all ten years ago. Now, on this particular evening, Kamala, who usually was a willing listener to her son's tales of his *kabaddi* exploits, was preoccupied. While Raju and Lakshmi were playing *kabaddi*, Kamala had gone to the temple to argue with Bikshu. The arguments were all the same. Possessed of a deeply spiritual nature, Kamala was determined to gain the insights that would allow her to understand the world—Lord Shiva's dance—and where she could fit in with this journey of human souls through many lives and places, all in the rhythm of the cosmic dance of Lord Shiva. She wanted to understand so she could show the way to others, especially to her dear son, and husband, and grandfather—if they were still alive. To do this, however, she would have to study to become a *sannyasi*—the spiritually enlightened ones or wise sages—to whom others turned for spiritual guidance. Studying, Kamala had done aplenty, but *sannyasis* were all men.

Indeed, again today Bikshu told her, "Kamala, if only you were a man, you could be a *sannyasi* and obtain *moksha,* and stay in heaven with Lord Shiva—and be released from the long cycle of rebirths here on earth."

Kamala had a quick retort. "Where in Holy Hindu Scripture, good Bikshu, does it say a woman cannot become a *sannyasi?*"

As usual in their arguments, Bikshu was forced to admit he could not find such a verse. He again admitted there had been women rulers, *Ranis,* or queens, but Bikshu remained adamant that Lord Shiva insisted only men could gain the status of a *sannyasi.* With a twinkle in his eye, Bikshu suggested the path to becoming a man, for a woman, was through the life of a sacred cow.

Indignant, Kamala stomped her feet. "You're joking!"

Bikshu became evasive. "We'll see. Who knows how the wheel of the dance really turns? Sometimes things that seem just fine with Lord Shiva can seem a little strange to us."

"A little strange, you say," Kamala replied. "You have always said that I am your best student, but that I simply cannot be a *sannyasi* as a woman. Now you are telling me that I should be happy to be a cow. I have no intention of becoming a cow."

Bikshu laughed and countered, "I didn't say you should be happy, but it is a means to an end. Besides, a cow's life is not all bad, and there is much to be learned from a sacred cow in anyone's journey."

"Well, not mine," Kamala retorted.

Bikshu persisted. "Remember this as well, Kamala. Lord Shiva's time runs in a different rhythm from ours. We live our lives in order: from birth through life to death. But on the heavenly side of his dance, we can return to earthly life at different stages: as a new-born babe, as a grown-up in mid-life, or as someone elderly. I say this because your soul and Raju's soul are bound to a common path of *samsara* for your family."

"How can that be?" Kamala objected. "My family is so scattered, and Raju is just a boy."

"Well, then, it's time to bring your souls together. Kamala, the time for your rebirth is near. Come with me to the Lotus Pond."

Kamala was taken aback by the suddenness of this revelation. As they walked to the pond, the enormity of what was to happen slowly sunk in. But when they came to the pond, Kamala became frivolous. "If this is my time, may I ask Lord Shiva for a small favor?"

"What is it?"

'Ever since Raju was born, I have had this orange mole under my right eye. Could you ask Lord Shiva to make it disappear in my next life? I swear the thing gives me headaches. When I have them, I sometimes hallucinate into thinking I am a swan, if you can believe it."

Bikshu did not reply at first. Instead, he walked into the pond and picked up a lotus flower. "As you know, your name Kamala here in North India means lotus, the flower of *samsara*. But it also has a second meaning. In the languages of South India, Kamala means tangerine, a very orange-colored fruit."

"I didn't know that," Kamala replied. "But what's the point?"

Bikshu spread apart the petals of the lotus flower in his hand. "At the base of the lotus flower is a black pod with hundreds of little orange seeds spurting from it. These are the seeds of *samsara*— and your special sign of remembrance. Go home now, Kamala. Fix your son a special meal. Your journey begins."

Kamala strode from the temple deep in thought.

On this particular evening, Kamala fixed Raju his favorite meal, lamb *biryani*, an expensive rice and curry dish. After the meal, Kamala related to Raju what the priest had told her. "One way or another, Raju, it appears that the time for rebirth is upon me. Before this happens, I need to tell you about your father."

Raju, who had been suppressing a yawn of contentment from his delicious meal, grew instantly alert. "My father. What about my father?"

"Your father, Raman Pandu, was a captain in the Palace Guard. For some reason," Kamala went on, "he lost favor with the king. Shortly after your birth, he was sent on a dangerous mission to capture Afghan raiders who had been preying on the roads to the north. He never returned, so he only saw you as a newborn. In five years he was presumed to be dead, and the king provided us with a small pension. I know he loved you very much—he probably still does," she slipped.

Raju gasped. "What!? Is father still alive?"

Kamala was careful in her reply. "I have been told he miraculously survived a vicious ambush of his men by Afghans, and he is in the northern mountains in search of your grandfather, the legendary Indra Singh. Many times, I have told you that this supposed legend is really my father."

"Yes, Mother, but I never believed you before."

Kamala smiled. Then she drew herself up in a business-like manner. "When the moment for my rebirth comes, you are to go to Bikshu, who will have further instructions for you about Lord Shiva's plans."

"Don't worry, Mother," Raju consoled her. "You'll be all right."

"Thanks to you, son, I know I will," was her strange reply. Even more strange was her parting instruction. "And, Raju, when my time comes, our neighbor will have a packet for you to give to your future wife as a gift from me."

The next day, when he returned home from school, Raju saw a plume of smoke rising above his street. When he drew nearer, the plume of smoke revealed a brilliant orange flame devouring his home. Neighbors firmly turned Raju away. One of them came up to him with a packet and told him, "Raju, here is your mother's necklace."

Chapter 5

The Temple Visit

Kamala's funeral ceremony was held at the palace temple on the banks of the sacred River Ganges. Raju entered the temple in a daze, as if it were his first time. He hardly noticed its square shape with its interior halls. But he did take notice of all the statues of favorite gods and goddesses. He also recognized some of the priests who were assisting individual worshipers do *puja*, or the proper rites for their prayers. He looked back at the front gate with a classic cast bronze statue of Lord Shiva welcoming the worshipers with his cosmic dance. It was an impressive statue, even from the back. His eyes turned to the middle of the temple with its large open pool for ceremonial washings before devotees entered the halls to do their *puja*. As he walked to the back of the temple, he took in the huge tower, called a *gopuram*, crawling with carvings of all the gods and goddesses that were part of Lord Shiva's story. Underneath the *gopuram*, he became nervous as he walked through the passageway leading to the riverbank. From the passageway he saw the burning *ghats* holding the pyres or platforms for the cremation of dead bodies. Raju stepped out from the temple and cringed.

Two priests met Raju and ushered him to these burning *ghats*. Waiting for him was a funeral pyre of neatly stacked logs cradling Kamala's body in a white cotton shroud. Bikshu stood at the head of the funeral pyre and greeted Raju. "It is good to see you, Raju. I am so sorry about your mother's sudden passing. It was a cooking fire in the kitchen, and everything was burned to ashes so quickly your mother did not suffer. In fact, neighbors came in time to see to it that she died from the smoke, not the flames. In any case, fire is the noble way for a high-born soul to die. She is freed from her body more quickly for her ascent to the gods," Bikshu said, trying to comfort Raju who sobbed in sorrow.

Raju was surprised to see at the foot of the funeral pyre a man with a hood that covered most of his face, except for a pair of eyes fixed on Raju. Raju wiped his tears and looked away. As the surviving son, and with no father, it was Raju's duty to place the burning torch on the pyre. A sudden breeze lit up the pyre, and the logs crackled in the flames that consumed the body of Kamala. All the while, Bikshu recited *mantras* of deliverance for the soul of Kamala. Raju also noticed when the shroud was engulfed in flames, tears streamed down the face of the hooded man. *"Who is he?"* Raju thought.

Later in the day, after the flames had completely consumed the pyre, a priest shoveled the ashes into a silver bucket. Bikshu took the bucket and cast the ashes into the sacred River Ganges. As the ashes slowly dissolved in the river's current, Bikshu declared, "Kamala, we release your soul to its chosen path."

Bikshu then summoned Raju to follow him to the temple. There he took Raju to a private room with an idol of the Dancing Shiva. Bikshu asked the boy what he saw. Raju described the God standing on one foot with the other bent in a dancing pose, his four arms struck into four different poses (one of which daintily held a lily), and his body divided into male and female halves—all surrounded by a circle of fire. The priest swept his hand around the circle and told Raju, "We are all bound by this fiery circle in a chain of birth and re-birth, and only the gods could free us from this "chain of serial life" by the gift of *moksha*, or release.

Bikshu then described the path of Kamala's soul from its ascent from the ashes of her corpse beside the River Ganges. It rose, with the souls of many other heavenly pilgrims, to a large meadow at the foot of Mount Meru. At the far end of the meadow stood a small hillock on which three gods sat on the throne of judgment: Brahma, Vishnu, and Shiva who represented the Past, Present, and Future, which was the cycle of time that bound all mortals.

"Wait a minute. Hold on," uttered Raju. "This is way beyond my understanding.

So, we are all in this circle. Then what happens?"

"The goal is to escape all this, which is *moksha*, when you get to stay with the gods on Mount Meru forever. At the end of one life, you must choose another. And these choices determine your path to *moksha*," explained Bikshu.

"How?" asked Raju.

"Let us go back to our story of Kamala coming to the throne of judgment. There each soul is ushered one-by-one before it and each soul is assigned a new life. The soul could ask for a particular one, but it would be bound by the memory of just his one previous life, and what it remembered as good and desirable from that one experience. The gods, of course, might modify some of the choices based on the merit, or lack of it, of the previous life."

Bikshu continued. "A few, a very few, are pulled aside and granted *moksha*, or release, and are led up Mount Meru to join the gods in the heavens. For most, however, whose choices are based on remembering one life at a time, their cycle of lives continues. They are plunged into the River of Forgetfulness, where they forget everything about this immortal world they have just visited, and are plunged down to the earth again, with a shooting star signifying each new birth—as Lord Shiva dances on.

Raju sighed. "I don't know about Mother, but I don't see how I could make the right choice."

Having provided this general description to a wondering Raju, Bikshu suddenly became personal. "Let us bring this cosmic wheel down to your life, Raju. For a few, there is a shorter path. These are the ones who retain the gift of remembrance. These few remember many of their previous lives, not just the one they have just lived. These are the ones that can come before the throne of judgment and recall the string of lives the dancing Shiva has given them. They will know what to ask for to obtain release because they can recall the cosmic plan of their soul—and what was good and what was bad about their previous lives. Armed with this prior knowledge, they can be sent back to life for a short visit to fulfill one final purpose for their release. Usually, these few will have an identifying mark or characteristic that serves as a beacon of remembrance of this plan through the stormy journey around the base of Mount Meru. Kamala's mark, of course, is her orange mole. You, Raju, as well are marked for remembrance. But yours is not a visible one."

Bikshu turned, as if he had forgotten something. "There is one more thing about these soul journeys. Animals can be part of these journeys, animals like swans, snakes, monkeys, and cows. These are sacred because they can travel on the paths of human souls. Swans are part of the path of beauty and love because they mate for life. Snakes may be dangerous, but they are also very wise, and can help those struggling to understand their souls. Monkeys look human because they are almost human. Souls who want to recover human compassion can start this path through the life of a monkey. Most sacred of all, of course, is the cow."

"Yes," said Raju. "I never knew why the cow is so sacred. Mother would get furious at me if I so much as touched one. Because they are sacred, everyone gives them food, or lets them chew the grass in their fields. They just sit around all day just eating and being lazy. What makes this sacred?"

"It is their contentment," Bikshu replied. "For those souls whose path needs a big change from their last life, they might need a life that can see beyond the change. Cows see only unity, the oneness of everything. They don't see all the differences that divide us in life."

"I don't understand a word you are saying," said Raju.

Bikshu smiled, "You will, Raju. You will."

Bikshu then rose and put his hands on the boy's shoulders. "It is time now for you to start your journey in Shiva's dance." The priest went to a chest and drew out a small ebony box. He handed it to the boy. "You will need to take this with you. Open the box," he softly commanded.

Raju pulled out the orange silk turban cloth inside the box. He gasped. From it tumbled the brilliant Golconda Diamond.

Bikshu let the shock of this sight settle for a bit, then began. "To see your Mother again, you must follow my instructions closely. Your grandfather is, as you know, Indra Singh, the former commander of the Palace Guard, who is bound by a terrible vow: that he will not return to the palace unless he has the missing diamond in his hand—the diamond you now have in your hand. The terrible part of the vow is that without the diamond, Indra Singh will be executed. The night before he set out on his quest for the diamond, he related this vow to his tearful wife, Parvati. Meanwhile, his daughter, your mother Kamala, had become pregnant, and I attended the birth of the child—you. After you were born, she started a fearful retching, and she was brought to me for a final blessing. I sent everyone out, so I could be alone with your mother. I began to pray, and Lord Shiva appeared to me in a vision with an urgent command and instruction:

Slap Kamala's back. Take what comes out—the Golconda Diamond—and do not show it to anyone. Give it to her son at the appropriate time. Send him to Indra Singh, along with a cow that I shall provide. Command the boy NOT to show him or anyone else the diamond until the cow dies.

Raju, I took the diamond and gave Kaamla back to you, her child. Until today, I have never shown the diamond to anybody. Neither your mother nor your father ever knew it had come to the temple. As you can probably guess, your mother, Kamala, was the swan who swallowed the diamond, and you were her little cygnet, Babu. Both of you were reborn, then, as a mother and child. Raju, you must always remember this as I send you off on the next leg of your soul's journey."

"What I will remember," mused Raju, "is that I was a little swan that never got to grow up into a beautiful big swan."

"Remember, also, that you were a little swan that adored his mother and followed her everywhere—which is still your destiny," Bikshu interrupted. "So, son, let me tell you what you must do to follow Lord Shiva's divine instruction. First, I am sending you to your grandfather, who leads a band of good men in the mountains far to the north. I believe it is called Kafiristan, the land of the poor. Kafiristan is just beyond the borders of the Kingdom of Vijayapura, in the Himalaya Mountains. It is strategically located near the pilgrimage route to Mount Meru and along the Royal Road leading out of India into Afghanistan."

"Indra Singh set up Kafiristan as a trap. Rather than search the lands of each of the *rajas* of

King Chandra Gupta's court for the diamond, he thought he could intercept and entertain these *rajas* on their pilgrimages or out-of-country trips to see if they either had the diamond, or knew who did. A little less pleasantly, by setting up Kafiristan as a kingdom to help the poor, he might even kidnap a *raja* or two high on his suspect list and shake them down for the diamond as a 'contribution' to the poor. As you can see, none of this has worked."

"This is all too much," Raju protested. "If nothing is working, why don't I just not bother and become a bull frog and croak away at the swans in the lake. Besides, what you ask will take way too long—forever!"

Bikshu became impatient. "Your forever is just a little drop of water in Lord Shiva's bucket. You've got to start thinking beyond your life. If you don't, you will make mistakes that will destroy your path. Here is your situation and what you must do:

King Chandra Gupta has become suspicious of Kafiristan. He still doesn't realize that Indra Singh is its leader. Even worse, since he does not know the whereabouts of Indra Singh, he has become suspicious that he has turned traitor and is in league with a faction of his court *rajas*, or even teamed up with the notorious Haider Ali of Golconda. I will keep stalling King Chandra Gupta from mounting a military mission against Kafiristan. Now that you have the diamond, we can bring this journey to a conclusion."

Raju looked bewildered.

Bikshu went on. "Don't worry about all this right now. Back to Lord Shiva's instruction: you are going to Kafiristan, to be sure, but do not undertake the journey until the cow that was at your home gives birth.

"Hey!" interrupted Raju, "Where is that cow? I need her milk."

"I took her to the temple when your mother died. She will give birth to a calf soon," Bikshu quietly replied. "After the calf is weaned, you are to take it with you to Kafiristan. While you are there, Learn everything you can from your grandfather. He is a great warrior and nearly a *sannyasi* himself. Finally—and most important of all—do not show anyone or tell anyone about the diamond until the calf dies—that especially includes your grandfather and everyone else you come to know in Kafiristan."

"What!" exclaimed Raju. "That stupid calf could live ten years—or more! Why can't I just go to Kafiristan right now, without the calf, give the diamond to my grandfather, and let him return to the palace so everyone can live happily ever after?"

Bikshu stared at Raju before offering a stern reply. "Because no one will live happily ever after. Not you. Not your mother. Not your father. Not your grandfather. Not even King Chandra Gupta or Lakshmi or your children, for that matter. For all these souls to reach their happily-ever-afters, everything depends on the diamond, and you doing the right thing with it. In your hands, Raju, lies the destinies of all these souls. Follow Lord Shiva's instruction, and all of them will attain *moksha*, and an eternity of happiness with the gods."

"Do not let the pull of one life—yours, your grandfather's, your father's—break the rhythm of Lord Shiva's dance. Fall off from the instruction, and all these souls, whose destinies are joined together by spiritual signs and remembrances, will be cast out and become lost in the abyss of outer space. But Lord Shiva knew what he was doing when he ordained that you were to be the key to this family's *moksha*. You have a gift and strength you don't yet realize." Bikshu's tone became deadly serious. "Hold on to this, Raju, no matter what: Do not show the diamond to anyone until the calf dies. This is Lord Shiva's divine instruction."

CHAPTER 6

THE FOREST

A little over nine months later, Raju's cow was ready to deliver her calf. A messenger from Bikshu escorted Raju to the temple for the delivery. He was surprised by the "reception committee" that awaited him. Bikshu, of course, was there, but so also was the strange man who was at Kamala's funeral pyre. The real surprise was Lakshmi.

Bikshu spoke before Raju could say anything. "I need this man here, Raju, because I need a strong man who has experience with birthing calves to help me. Also, this calf will be his spiritual responsibility. That's why the cow is giving birth at the temple."

"And Lakshmi?" Raju asked, pleased to see her.

"Lakshmi is also here for the spiritual occasion. She will offer a special blessing for the calf," Bikshu explained.

"But Lakshmi is a girl," Raju protested.

"And your mother, Kamala, was a woman," was Bikshu's puzzling reply.

None of this made sense to Raju, but he blushed when Lakshmi smiled and stuck out her tongue at him.

Someone who also took note of Lakshmi's gesture was King Chandra Gupta, who had followed her to the temple. The king turned to Bikshu. "What is going on?"

What was going on was that he was not sure what to make of this newly observed friendship between his daughter and Raju.

Nobody noticed how quickly the strange man hid himself when the king arrived.

Bikshu's reply broke up the king's thoughts. "Oh, my king, Raju has brought the cow for delivery at the temple because the calf that will be born has a role to play in Lord Shiva's dance that involves Raju—and the others."

"The others?" the king raised his brow.

"The calf will be a female, and I thought it fitting that Lakshmi offer a blessing for the cow. She and Raju are *kabaddi* teammates."

The king really was confused now. He tried to gain control of the situation. "Continue on with this delivery, Bikshu. Lakshmi, be sure to be back at the palace before dinner." With this, the king strode off to the palace.

The delivery of the calf proved difficult. The strange man reappeared and took over the delivery from Bikshu. As sometimes happened during these deliveries, the calf's head had to be turned. When the calf was born, the right side of her face was damaged as a result, creating what would become a permanent scar. When Raju saw the calf, he pointed to the hurt and exclaimed, "Ooh! What a *debba*." From then on, she was Debba.

Once the calf was cleaned and able to stand, Bikshu handed Lakshmi a sheet of paper. "Put your hand on Debba's forehead and read this."

Lakshmi went up to the calf and read:

"Debba, may your journey be true, and your life follow

Lord Shiva's appointed path. May Raju be true to his vow

as Lakshmi awaits her turn on the wheel of Lord Shiva's

dance."

Lakshmi and Raju asked in unison, "What does this blessing mean?"

"Everyone is part of the story of Lord Shiva's dance." Bikshu's answer explained nothing to the confused pair.

With the calf cleaned, named, and blessed, Bikshu told Raju he should get ready for his journey to find his grandfather. He directed Raju to go home, gather his luggage, and meet Debba the calf at the temple. When Raju arrived the next day, the priest introduced him to the man who had helped them with the birth of the calf. "This is 'Namar,' Raju, and he will guide you to Indra Singh's little land of Kafiristan. Now remember what I said about the calf."

"Right," Raju replied.

Namar looked puzzled, but Raju just shrugged his shoulders.

Raju turned to Bikshu. "Just a minute. I'd…well, I'd…like to see Lakshmi before we leave."

Bikshu smiled. "I thought of that and sent word to the palace."

No sooner had he said this than Lakshmi burst into the temple courtyard. "Raju, where are you going?"

Raju did not know how to respond. "Well…"

Bikshu interrupted to prevent Raju from saying anything about the diamond. "Raju, the calf, and this man here are undertaking a spiritual quest so something pure may be found and revealed, so a soul may become wise, and so a son's love may put the wheel of Lord Shiva's dance on a proper path to *moksha.*"

"This is pretty much the truth," Bikshu thought.

Almost reading his mind, Lakshmi stomped her feet. "This is pretty much nothing but a riddle."

"Yes, Lakshmi, but you are part of the riddle's dance as well," Bikshu said.

"How so?" asked Lakshmi.

Raju had been listening to the conversation waiting to cut in. "I'll show you, Lakshmi. I have a gift for you." From his large cloth *sanchi* (satchel), which was packed for his trip, he took out a velvet purse, and handed it to her. "This is for you. Open it."

Lakshmi opened the purse and pulled out Kamala's glistening diamond necklace. She gasped, and then turned beet red. "Raju, when a man gives a woman a valuable necklace like this, it means they intend to be married. We are only ten years old. Well, I just turned eleven, so I am a bit older than you."

"It's my mother's necklace. A few days before she died, Mother told me that the necklace was for me to pass on to my wife. I know you are the one she meant it for. You are part of our story. Since we are still young, the necklace is a promise. I will marry you when I return from this journey," Raju said.

"How long is this journey going to take?"

"Could be years."

"Years, how many years?"

"I don't know. Not that many. We will still be young enough when I get back."

Raju turned serious. "I am taking this journey under a sacred promise. Now I have a promise to ask of you."

"And that is?" asked Lakshmi.

"Do not tell your father, the king, about this necklace, and do not wear it until I see you again," Raju insisted.

Lakshmi's curiosity, and anticipation, were really aroused now. "When I see you again, and I wear the necklace, does that mean we will get married?"

Raju's reply was firm. "If the necklace is around your neck, we will get married, yes. If it is not, I will understand you have selected another man for a husband."

Lakshmi blushed and changed the subject. "What am I supposed to tell my father about where you are going? He is going to wonder why I have no more *kabaddi* stories about you."

Bikshu looked at Raju with alarm. Raju tried to send Bikshu a look of reassurance, as he gravely turned to Lakshmi. "Tell him that Raju won't be playing *kabaddi* at the temple anymore. With his mother's death, he has gone to live with—distant—relatives. But when he is grown, he hopes to return to serve the king."

Bikshu smiled.

Lakshmi's eyes teared up a little. "Then, I'll see you when I see you."

"Yes," Raju replied. "I'll see you when I see you."

Lakshmi walked through the temple on her way out.

"All right, Raju," Bikshu said, "You and Namar and the calf need to start your journey. Follow Namar wherever you go, and he will take care of you—and Debba. Don't let her out of your sight—nor your *sanchi*."

So, the boy, the cow, and Namar set off. Raju kept the ebony box with the diamond hidden in the bottom of his *sanchi*.

On the way out of the temple, they crossed through the middle of the *kabaddi* court. Out of nowhere, Lakshmi dashed across the court screaming *"kabaddi, kabaddi, kabaddi."* Kamala's diamond necklace shimmered at her throat. She grabbed Raju and held him tight. Reflexively, Raju took a breath and shouted his own *"kabaddi, kabaddi, kabaddi."*

To stop him, Lakshmi kissed him hard on the mouth, which made Raju lose his breath. "Got you," Lakshmi gloated, as Raju fell to the ground. Lakshmi ran off. At the gate she turned, smiled, and took off the necklace, held it up, and shouted, "Until then," and disappeared.

Raju picked himself up. Namar broke out in a smile that turned into a laugh, as Debba snorted.

Their journey took a month. They trekked over hot, dusty plains as they headed north to the mountains. The mountains rose above the dusty villages of Vijayapura, and the air became clearer—and colder. Settlements grew sparse. Soon they disappeared altogether, as the forests grew thicker and darker. Rivers and streams that were brown, dirty, and warm became clear, clean, and icy cold.

After one particularly thorny path, they stumbled onto a clearing. Opposite them rose a mountain ridge that rolled down to a black, rocky cliff that towered above them. Over this cliff tumbled a roaring waterfall whose waters lapped at their feet. The three stood transfixed by the majestic sight. Namar smiled and said, "This is it, our home in the forest. Put this coat over yourself and Debba and follow me." No sooner had Raju done this than a black speck in the sky flew down to them. As the bird closed in, Raju noticed the white wing feathers, just as he heard the familiar "caw, caw,

caw, *kabaddi, kabaddi, kabaddi,* caw, caw, caw." Raju now knew that Bikshu would know where they were.

"What is that?" demanded Namar.

"That," laughed Raju, "is the very annoying bird, Vijaya, Bikshu's magpie—and messenger."

After watching Vijaya fly away, they marched straight into the waterfall to a space where the waters parted underneath an overhanging rock. They burst through the falls into a dark corridor. Torches along the corridor beckoned them. Once they got to the torches, the tunnel bent into a gauntlet of lights and shadowy figures. A few turns later, the trio came upon a full chamber of lights. In the middle of the chamber, hanging from the ceiling like a grand chandelier, was an image of Shiva twisting slowly in the air. The chamber was full of men who looked like outlaws to Raju.

There was a long table with a white cloth set up on a rock dais. A white-bearded man, still of firm build, shouted from the head of the table. "Welcome, grandson. I am Indra Singh, your grandfather. The man who has been traveling with you, Namar, is actually Raman Pandu. We reversed his name to fool you. He is my right-hand man— and he is also your father. We could not let your father identify himself to you for fear the king would find out and force me to return to his court without the diamond, thereby making me fulfill my vow of killing myself. We have tried to keep up with your activities through Bikshu, who has sent you to our care."

Though still grief-stricken by his mother's death, Raju was delighted to be reunited with his father and grandfather.

He grew to adulthood under their care. Raju learned that the two men pledged their full loyalty to King Chandra Gupta, while they continued their quest for the missing diamond. In the ten years before Raju's arrival, they had checked each of the *rajas* who ruled the fiefs and principalities of Chandra Gupta's kingdom, and found they were all innocent. All still professed their loyalty, and none of them had the diamond. The two men kept their labors secret because they did not want to have to return to the palace without the diamond, lest their lives be forfeited.

One difficult task lay ahead: the long-dreaded quest and long-delayed search of the original home of the diamond, the kingdom of Golconda. They had saved this search for last because it would be the most difficult, and the most consequential. It would be difficult because it was, after all, another kingdom, and the search would require both stealth and a strong force. But it was the consequences they feared. To fail to find the diamond there would mean the quest was over, and they had failed. In this eventuality, they had agreed to return to Vijayapura and bear the terrible consequences of Indra Singh's oath. To succeed, on the other hand, by finally finding the diamond in Golconda, would confirm the king's suspicion of treachery, and a major war would follow as sure as the next bend in the sacred River Ganges'

While his grandfather and father stewed, Raju squirmed in the agony of his secret knowledge and possession. Within easy reach, buried in the bottom of his *sanchi*, lay the end of their quest—except for Lord Shiva's divine prohibition of this revelation until the death of Debba—who remained playfully alive.

In the meantime, Indra Singh and Raman Pandu had set up a forest kingdom they called Kafiristan, the land of the poor. Though loyal to their king, Chandra Gupta, whose authority was weak in this remote region, they served the poor citizens of this land, regardless of which landlord, money lender, or royal official they had to "tax" to ease the burdens of their "subjects." Some of their more brazen taxations had come to the attention of the king, and Chandra Gupta occasionally expressed an interest in finding out more about this exotic kingdom of outlaws. Bikshu, however, was always able to deflect the king's attention to other problems.

CHAPTER 7

THE BLACK SWAN

Over the next eight years, Raju grew to manhood under the instruction of his two mentors, or *gurus*, as such teachers are called in India: Indra Singh, his grandfather, and Raman Pandu, his father. Raju soon discovered they had opposite natures. Indra Singh was the spiritual one, while his father was a fearless and skilled warrior.

His daily routine settled into sessions of long talks with Indra Singh in the mornings. After lunch, Raman Pandu would try to teach him the skills of a soldier: wielding a sword, hurling a lance, swinging a mace, and, eventually, the special skill of archery. These military instructions became somewhat erratic because Raman Pandu was often away on secret scouting missions trying to pinpoint where the missing diamond might be in Golconda before they launched any full-scale raid to recover the invaluable jewel. These missions of his father were agonizing to Raju. The diamond seemed to burn in his *sanchi* even as Lord Shiva's instruction that he had to wait until Debba's death always held him in check.

In fact, in Raju's lessons with Indra Singh, Debba, now a full-grown cow, was always present, and seemed more interested in what Indra Singh was talking about than Raju. Whenever Indra Singh used the phrase, "Lord Shiva's dance," Debba rolled her head in a complete circle, as if she were nodding in agreement. Indra Singh was teaching Raju about the heroes of India's famous epic, *The Mahabharata.* This was the story about the cosmic battle between the heroic five Pandava brothers versus their notorious Kuru cousins. It was all too involved for Raju, and his attention often wandered.

But two stories caught his attention: one good, the other he thought was bad. The good story was really a book inserted in the middle of *The Mahabharata* called *The Bhagavad Gita*—The Song of God. It was about another way or passage to *moksha*, or the release to heaven.

"So, let me tell you about this other path, Raju," Indra Sing began.

"I know, I know, there are many paths to *moksha*. Who's to know what's best?" Raju replied wearily.

Indra Singh grew emphatic. "Well, this is the path that applies especially to you—and to us, your family,"

Raju perked up. He remembered something like this from Bikshu.

"Most people follow paths of many lives, but when families stay together bound by their love for each other and for God, Lord Shiva is pleased to grant them, together, a shorter path: the path of love. In the *Gita*, this is what God offered the Pandava hero, Arjuna." Indra Singh closed his eyes and recited from memory:

> "Give me your whole heart,
> Love and adore me, Worship
> me always, Bow to me only, And
> you shall find me... For I will
> save you From sin and from the
> bondage (Of many lives)."

"I added the last line," Indra Singh explained, "because the path of love will bring us all into the presence of Lord Shiva together sooner."

Debba perked up at this. She snorted, turned her head very deliberately in a full circle, and then looked sharply at Raju.

Raju patted the cow's head and said, "I think you know more about this than I do, Debba."

Indra Singh cut in, "You, Raju, are the key. Your love—and something else I can't quite put my fingers on yet—are the links between Kamala, Raman Pandu, me, King Chandra Gupta, and Lakshmi—and let's not forget the swans."

Raju became uncomfortable. He was afraid that Indra Singh was getting close to the secret he could not reveal—the diamond in his *sanchi*. He bit his lip as he got up nervously and beckoned to Debba. "Come on, Debba, let's get some lunch. All this loving is getting me hungry."

Indra Singh regarded the pair as they left. Another thing he could not put his fingers on was Debba. "What's with this cow?" he mused. "Why is she even with us, and hanging around us all so closely? Bikshu told Raman we are to watch over her and keep her close until she dies. That could be awhile. She's a pretty lively cow."

The other story always upset Raju. It was about the moral dilemma faced by the hero Bhima. On the eve of the climactic event of *The Mahabharata*, the seventeen-day battle between the rival clans and their allied gods, Bhima was told by Lord Shiva that to preserve the good order of the universe and the favorable outcome to this battle, Bhima would have to cheat. With great reluctance he did, and the evil Kuru clan went down to defeat.

"That's simply not fair," was Raju's constant reply every time he heard the story.

Indra Singh was always firm in his reply. "When the gods command, their orders are for greater reasons than we humans can see." Today, Indra Singh added a command of his own. "Even if we see something in front of us that from a human perspective seems to be wrong, we still, always, have to obey the gods. Do not forget this, Raju, because I feel very strongly that you will be tested, and the fate of our family will be in your hands."

As if in agreement, Debba circled her head again, but Raju squirmed in the agony of his secret promise. With all these moral dilemmas Indra Singh kept tossing up, Raju became eager to get away to the military practice field with his father in the afternoon. But this field had its bumps as well. Raman Pandu was a military genius, but not much of a teacher.

Raju tried the sword, but he proved too slow swinging it. Despite Raju's skill at *kabaddi*, and from it, wrestling, the mace was too heavy. When he tried to hurl the spear, Raju could not keep his balance. Raman Pandu instinctively mastered all these weapons, but he could not break down the use of these weapons into teachable steps for Raju.

And Debba kept getting in the way. All these practices with weapons seemed like an invitation for the cow. She would frolic with Raman Pandu butting him in the side, and even knocking him down. Then she'd shake her head and lick him in the face. Naturally, this ruined the seriousness of these lessons, but his father seemed to enjoy it. The three would roll on the ground in laughter, but Raju was not learning how to be a good soldier.

Also, as the years sped by, Indra Singh sent Raman Pandu on more and more missions. Some were to block scouting parties sent by King Chandra Gupta to learn more about Kafiristan and whether the rumors were true that Indra Singh was the leader of this little forest kingdom. But others were secret forays into Golconda to pinpoint where the diamond might be hidden in this southern land. Finally, at about the fifth or sixth year of this frustrating training, Raju simply asked, "Father, just tell me your secret."

Raman lit up at this. "It is the black swan, Raja," he replied. "I always keep him with me in my heart.

I always remember him: what he said and what he could see."

"Tell me about him, Father, then I can learn," Raju said.

For the first time Raman seemed to enjoy talking. "When I was sent off by King Chandra Gupta as a captain of the Palace Guard to drive out the Afghan raiders, I was headstrong and angry. It angered me that the king did not trust me because of my marriage to Kamala, Indra Singh's daughter. He said that no matter what happened on this mission, I could not return to the palace until news came of the success or failure of Indra Singh's mission. I wanted to win back the king's favor with a great triumph. I was fearless in battle but blinded by pride. This nearly led to disaster."

"As we journeyed to the far western mountains, the *Hindu Kush*, leading to the homeland of these Afghan raiders, we came to a stream flowing into a forest. Instead of sending out scouting parties,

I ordered my men to charge into the forest immediately so we could surprise the raiders whom I knew were waiting for us. Unfortunately, we were the ones surprised. As soon as we entered the forest, we were attacked from all sides. My chariot struck a boulder, and I fell to the ground. I got up and formed the survivors into a circle, and we put up a stubborn defense. But there were too many, and we retreated along a stream that led to a waterfall of a thousand feet. Finally, the company of bodyguards around me surrendered, and I decided to jump over the falls and entrust my fate to Lord Shiva."

"As it happened, there was a raging wind swirling around these cliffs. I was wearing a cape, and I tried desperatcly to fashion it into a sail. But I was too heavy. As my futile attempts at sailing were degenerating into an outright fall, a huge black swan swooshed under me, and with his strong wings beating the air, he tried to cushion my fall.

Somehow it managed to slow my descent into a survivable crash into the river at the bottom of the waterfalls. Clearly, Lord Shiva had sent this swan to save me. Ever since, I have pledged my life to his service—and the king's, of course."

"Something about the swan was familiar. Somehow, in the blow from the fall, I found I could understand his speech. Or he could understand mine. I do not know, but the swan said it was Shiva's gift. I was still dazed. But he impressed upon me that with this gift of bird speech I could call on birds, during battles, to give me an air borne view of the battlefield. Once I understood the importance of this gift, the black swan asked me if I would help him discover the fate of his mate and cygnet."

"He settled down next to me and told me of his beautiful white swan and a devoted little cygnet that shared a lake with him on the grounds of the Vijayapura palace. It became time to teach the cygnet how to fly—a man's job—and he flew off in search of a high place for these lessons. Indeed, he came to this very place, which was farther away than he intended. When he returned to the lake, he could not find them."

"Glancing at his leg, I recognized the bracelet King Chandra Gupta had put there with the Vijayapura coat-of-arms on it. I told him his wife was Rani, the king's favorite swan, and both Rani and his cygnet had somehow drowned. No one seemed to know how, but the temple priest, Bikshu, had given them a funeral fit for royalty. In fact, just before I left on this mission, I visited Bikshu to secure his blessing. He prophesied that my fate would be in the hands of the black swan, Raja-you. Indeed, when I looked down over the waterfalls and saw you flying below me, it was the prophecy that inspired me to jump from the cliff. The black swan stood up and raised his neck to its full height and looked down on me."

"Then our destinies are truly joined," he said. Before leaving me, he promised, "With my family gone, I will fly up to Mount Meru to join them. One day, I will return to help you in a big battle. In the meantime, you can call on other birds, talk to them, and receive the gift of seeing your battles from the air.'"

"This gift, Raju, has been with me ever since, and that is my secret."

This story gave Raju just the opportunity he had been looking for. "So, Father, why don't you use the bird's speech approach with me—and just skip all the technical steps that get us nowhere—to teach me how to shoot the bow and arrow. There has always been a spirit—a gift, really—inside me that tells me the bow and arrow is my special weapon."

Raman Pandu looked at his son for a long time. Raju could see that his father was changing gears in his mind. "The bow, you know son, is the sacred weapon of kings and heroes. Maybe the bow is part of your destiny. Let us give it a try. But we need to pay a visit to your grandfather."

Indra Singh was not surprised by the visit. "I knew this moment was coming. You are destined for the bow and arrow, Raju. Lord Shiva's dance will take more steps in our journey with your mastery of it. Let us remember that the best archer of all time was the hero Arjuna in *The Mahabharata*. He was not taught the proper stance or the proper position for the right shoulder or how to grasp the bow. He was taught to look at his target, to see it, and to drive the image of the target deep into his mind—then let the arrow fly. He didn't aim the arrow. He let it fly to the image in his mind."

Indra Singh then led Raju and Raman Pandu to a storage room and opened it. In it was a bow and arrow the likes of which they had never seen. It was nearly as tall as Indra Singh. The bow was as thick as his grandfather's wrist, and the arrows were sleek and metallic. Indra Singh handed the bow to Raju. "This is my bow and arrow set that I will pass on to you. Try it out for size."

Raju looked at the bow with awe—and intimidation. The bow was taller than him, and much thicker than his wrists. He tried to string an arrow to the bow but could not. "It is too tight for me, grandfather."

Indra Singh smiled. "You are only sixteen now. In two more years, you will be big enough and tall enough to string it. But learn with this smaller one. It has the exact proportions and balance as the bigger one so what you learn on this bow, with more strength, you can easily transfer to the bigger one. The secret to archery is in the mind, not the arms."

And learn, Raju did. Under his father's guidance, he learned how to hit targets standing on the ground, hiding in the high branches of trees, and even on horseback. He learned how to hit targets in the clear under blazing sunlight, through forest foliage, and even in the darkness of night. All the while, Raju was growing bigger—and stronger.

One day in Raju's eighteenth year, Indra Singh came out to the field where Raju was practicing. The old man had his bow and arrow with him. He hailed Raju. "Here, son, take my bow and arrow and knock this orange off Debba's head." Raman Pandu became alarmed, but Debba stood stock still with the orange on her head. Raju strode confidently into position. He strung the bow easily this time.

Lord Shiva himself must have been watching because the whole world seemed to stop as Raju extended the bow in his left arm and pulled the arrow back to his shoulder with the right. Raju did not even see Debba, or even her head—just the image of the orange planted in his mind. The arrow flew, and the orange simply disappeared.

Indra Singh broke the silence. "The boy is ready, Raman. Take him with you on your next mission."

CHAPTER 8

GOLCONDA

The next mission came the very next day. Raman Pandu had posted lookouts along the river that formed the northern border of Vijayapura, which was also the southern limits of Kafiristan. The lookouts had sent word that a well-armed party had just crossed the river into Kafiristan. A horse was carrying a large strongbox. The horse was traveling next to a big man, also on horseback, sporting a fancy turban. In fact, he looked kingly, and the lookouts quickly concluded that he would make a good hostage. All told, there were about twenty in the party.

To Indra Singh, there was something odd about the openness of this group. He warned Raman. "Do not attack this group. Surround them and see what they want first. I think the group has been sent by King Chandra Gupta. We cannot afford to anger the king, especially since we have nothing to show for all these years in exile. This group has been sent to talk, not fight. Even worse, they are spies."

"All right," Raman replied. He turned to his men. "We'll have to do this differently. I'll send ravens out to locate this royal party, and then we will draw them into a forest glen where we can surround them. Do not do anything hasty. No one shoots first."

Indra Singh proved to be right. The ravens spotted the group moving in the open with no flanking guards or scouts clearing the way forward.

Finding a spot where the road passed between two boulders, Raman hid his men behind them to block their way. As soon as the turbaned man neared the boulders, Raman's men burst out in front to block the path, while others, including Raju, went around to the rear. The group was surrounded. But one boy, with a hood covering his face, broke free and ran down the road.

"Stop him, son," Raman ordered. "Don't let him get away."

Raju dashed after him.

Raman turned his attention to the turbaned man, and took the bridle of his horse,

"Welcome to Kafiristan, honored sir. Who are you that pays our remote little kingdom the courtesy of this visit? More to the point, why are you here?"

The turbaned man looked at Raman intently, and then a smile crossed his face. "Aha! You are Raman Pandu, the Captain of the Palace Guard who was sent on that suicide mission against Afghan raiders. If you succeeded, you were then supposed to find Indra Singh. I see you must have miraculously survived the raiders, but have you found Indra Singh?"

Raman was stunned at how much this man knew. He tried not to show it. "Not so fast, sir. You haven't answered my questions."

The turbaned man stood tall. "I am the Raja of Punjab, Mohan Singh, the largest domain in Vijayapura—well, after Golconda in the south. King Chandra Gupta sent me to find you and discover your progress, and your intentions."

"My progress and my intentions?" puzzled Raman. "You'll have to explain."

"You are obviously on a quest for something. I have no idea what it is, but King Chandra Gupta wants to know if you have found what you are looking for."

Raman could not hide the shock on his face and took a moment before replying. "It's hard to give you a direct answer. What we really seek is a kingdom nowhere in this world. It is a spiritual journey for our whole family. So, no, our search is not yet complete." As he spoke, he thought to himself that this was not a complete lie. After all, the missing diamond was just a key on the quest, not the ultimate goal or intention—but a very important key.

He abruptly changed the subject. "As for our intentions, we will merely take enough out of your strongbox to feed the next village down the road."

Raja Mohan Singh lifted the lid of the strongbox and flung it open. "See, there is nothing in the box."

Raman looked and saw that he was right. In disappointment, Raman lamented, "Our villages are going to be sad."

"No matter," the Raja retorted. He paused and then demanded: "Now, to business: you and Indra Singh have been gone from the court of Vijayapura for a long time. Are you two still loyal to King Chandra Gupta, or are you planning to overthrow him?"

Raman replied in a quiet voice. "I am glad to have this out in the open—and for this opportunity. Yes, we are loyal to the king. All these years, we have been on a mission for the king. Please tell King Chandra Gupta that we are nearly finished. One way or other, we will present ourselves to the king within a year."

Raja Mohan Singh lifted the reins of his horse. "Then my mission has been a success."

But Raman again still held the reins. "Hold on a minute. Did Bikshu bless your mission?"

"Bikshu never blesses any mission to find you renegades. Every time the king tries to send a mission to find you, Bikshu always blesses something else. But for this mission, Bikshu did not bless anything else, so we took his silence for a yes."

"I am glad you came," replied Raman, "but why did Bikshu relent?"

Grabbing back his bridle, Raja Mohan Singh replied, "I have no idea…Well, there is this mystery boy. Bikshu told us to take him along, but to never take off his mask, or ask who he is. He also said that if my mission were to succeed, the boy would be a large part of the reason. But I don't see how."

"It looks like my son Raju is about to find out."

Meanwhile, in his pursuit of the boy, Raju had lost track of him. As he looked all around, out of nowhere Vijaya flew down from the sky and fluttered over Raju's head screeching, "Caw, caw, caw, *kabaddi, kabaddi, kabaddi,* caw, caw, caw."

Completely bewildered, Raju shouted "What?" as he chased after Vijaya and what emerged as a dark shadow ahead of the bird. In a sprint, Raju gained on the shadow that was taking shape as the fleeing boy. The lad turned around, looked at Raju in surprise, gave a little laugh, and took off with an extra burst of speed. The road led into a patch of trees. Once among the trees, Raju lost sight of his prey. As he rounded a boulder, the lad leapt off it and grabbed Raju around the chest screaming, "*kabaddi, kabaddi, kabaddi.*"

Raju was better prepared this time and threw the lad off. In so doing, the lad's hood ripped free. Out flowed a stream of silky black hair. He grabbed her and shouted, "*Kabaddi, kabaddi, kabaddi,*" in return. "Lakshmi, what are you doing here?" Vijaya perched on a nearby branch and looked down at the pair with what seemed like fatherly satisfaction.

"I came to see you. I wanted to see you so badly. And Father wanted to find out about you and Raman Pandu and Indra Singh. So, I told Father that if I could go along on the mission, Raju would surely find me, and we could find out what Father wanted to know. Was I wrong, Raju? You just thought I was a boy when you chased me. Are you disappointed?" Lakshmi started to cry.

"Of course, I wanted to see you. This is the happiest day of my life," Raju said tenderly.

They had a lot of catching up to do, and they talked—and talked. After they talked themselves out, Lakshmi took a little velvet box from her skirt. "You gave me a necklace. I still have it, waiting for you. I didn't wear it today because I was afraid it might get stolen. Anyway, here is a token from me. Wear it when we see each other again."

Raju opened the box. Inside was a golden locket with a miniature painting of Lakshmi. He gasped at its beauty. "I will wear this locket around my neck always, Lakshmi. We are almost done here. We'll be together soon."

Lakshmi glowed at his promise but noticed Raju's look of worry. "What's wrong, Raju?" she asked.

"Before all this ends, something has to happen first—but let me worry about that. Surely Lord Shiva will let us return to court," Raju replied hopefully.

"Well, then, I'll see you when I see you," Lakshmi said.

Raju smiled. "I'll see you when I see you."

The pair returned to the group, and Lakshmi waved good-bye to Raju, as the Raja Mohan Singh party set off on their journey back to Vijayapura.

Because of Raman Pandu's promise to return to the king's court within a year, the mission to Golconda could no longer be put off. As they prepared, Indra Singh told Raman and Raju, "Since our destinies are linked, we must set out and see if the diamond is in Golconda. I tell you both, I fear if it is there, and I fear if it is not there. If it is there, of course, I fear a war. But if it is not there, I fear something worse than just losing our heads because then the diamond will be missing due to a moral defect in us, and we cannot obtain *moksha.*"

"I tell you, Raju, in this diamond lies the spiritual fortune of our family: of me, Raman Pandu, your mother Kamala, Lakshmi, Chandra Gupta, and you. I am convinced that, with the right understanding, Lord Shiva has ordered our release to happen together so we may climb Mount Meru as one family. But first we must undertake what I fear is a fruitless quest to Golconda. I say this because I think our good King Chandra Gupta is paranoid about this so-called diamond conspiracy. The answer to this missing diamond, I believe now, lies closer to home, very close."

Raju squirmed because the diamond was very close indeed. In fact, it was as close as the *sanchi* slung over his shoulder—and still no one knew. His grandfather was right: there was no need to go to Golconda. But Raju also knew the baby cow, now full grown, was not yet dead, and this was the one thing that still had to happen before he could let the diamond spill out of his *sanchi*. Taking all this in, Raju quietly said, "Let me come with you and grandfather. And let the cow, Debba, come too."

Raman protested, but Raju pleaded with Indra Singh. "Grandfather, just as Debba's and my coming here in the first place was fated by the gods, so is our participation in your final quest." Indra Singh looked at Raju for a long time and pondered Raju and Debba's first coming to them in the forest. He had come to understand that there was a cosmic dimension to their presence, and concluded, "If we are to go to Golconda, we will all go, even the cow. It is Lord Shiva's dance."

Indra Singh put together an expedition of just twenty men, with five of them mounted on horseback. The force had to be small because the secrecy of this desperate mission was critical. It must not be discovered by Haider Ali's troops because the incursion into Golconda territory was sure to trigger a war with Vijayapura. And, as they traveled through Vijayapura on their way, if their party were discovered by soldiers of Chandra Gupta, they were certain to be hauled back to the Vijayapura Court—without the diamond and their heads then put on the chopping block.

Before setting out, Raman sent out spies to scout the border of Golconda for the best place to sneak across. Since Golconda had been the central focus of the search for the diamond all along, spies had been sent out over the years to check out all the possible locations for the missing diamond. The palace in Hyderabad, the capital city of Golconda, had already been searched by paid informants—in the ladies' quarters, the Nawab's private apartments, all the armories, and every nook or cranny that had a vault. Even the mosques were searched. Only a few remained. It was time to concentrate on these last few sites.

On the expedition's journey to Golconda, Debba stayed close to Raju and Raman. In fact, they felt at home in her company. Raju had always been affectionate with the cow, and Raman would tenderly rub Debba behind her ears. "The three of you almost seem like a family," Indra Singh once observed. The father and son pretended not to notice.

Traveling by night, the trip to Golconda— south through the vast kingdom of Vijayapura, crossing the sacred River Ganges, and onto the Deccan Plateau even further south—took a month. Relying on the advice of their scouts, they crossed the Golconda border into a range of hills piled on gigantic boulders that struggled into the sunshine from a mat of thick jungle. Near the top, they settled in a large cave near a roaring waterfall that would drown out their noise. The mouth of the cave had a commanding view into the capital city of Hyderabad. The city was a sight: a web of narrow streets, bustling open bazaars for shopping and white marble mosques where Muslims worshipped. At the other end from their cave towered Nawab Haider Ali's palace with its fortified walls as thick as an elephant and its slender towers pointing to the sky like frozen spears. In the foreground was a green parade ground where the Nawab's powerful Arabian steeds raced each other in clouds of dust and rumbling noises of thunder. Mixed in with all these sights and sounds were the asphyxiating smells of human sweat, garbage, smoke, and food that rose out of the city in putrid waves.

Raju pinched his nose. "Phew! Do we have to go down there to find the diamond?"

Indra Singh laughed. "Vijayapura is no better, Raju. They are both cities with too many people. You've been with us in the forest too long. You've forgotten."

Meanwhile, spies trekked up to this mountain lair, one-by-one, with discouraging news. The diamond was not here. It was not there. It didn't seem to be anywhere. Then one night a spy came in who was sure he saw the diamond in a shrine beside a pond in the shadow of the palace. "I was able to sneak up to the shrine at midnight and look inside a window. From it, I saw a shaft of light reflecting off a moonbeam shining through another window across the room. At the point of these two rays of light was something small, bright, and shiny," he reported.

"That has to be it," Indra Singh and Raman Pandu said together.

"But it was very dark, and I couldn't be sure it was a diamond causing that light," protested the spy.

Indra Singh and Raman Pandu, however, were adamant, and they both insisted, "It has to be the diamond."

Raju instinctively raised his hand as if to stop them. The forbidding image of Lord Shiva that flashed in his mind forced him to lower his hand. But Indra Singh was quick to notice Raju's gesture. "Is there something on your mind, Raju?" he asked.

"No, no, you have to go through with this—carry it through to the end," Raju said in a lamenting voice.

Indra Singh was puzzled. "I am not sure I take your meaning, but we've got no choice but to go all out, and finish this, is that it?"

Raju heaved a sigh. "Yes, you must."

Scouts were immediately sent out to determine the numbers, dispositions, and rotations of the guards, the best routes for attack and withdrawal, and the best time to attack. Their reports were not encouraging. The shrine had a porch at the front door with a Muslim holy man seated on a mat, reading from the Holy *Qu'ran* by an oil lamp. The scouts reported that this reading went on all day and night, as the readers read in eight- hour shifts. The shrine was guarded by three tiers of guards encircling the shrine itself and the pond. Each tier had thirty men, for a total guard of about 100 men. To the side of the shrine was a small guard house where the Captain of the Guard stood. Near the Captain was a gong that could be used to summon the aid of the several hundred soldiers manning the palace walls. Clearly, the shrine was an important place. Where else could the diamond be? But any retrieval of this special jewel seemed hopeless.

Indra Singh took the news hard. In fact, on the trip south, he seemed more and more depressed every day. This news, now, was simply too much. "We should never have made this trip," he complained. "If we find the diamond here, and somehow make it back to Vijayapura, King Chandra Gupta will save our necks, but go to war against Golconda for stealing the diamond.

If we attack the shrine and fail—which seems inevitable—we will die for nothing, but Haider Ali will go to war thinking we are an attacking force from Vijayapura, which we are. If, by chance, we do succeed in taking the diamond without being detected by either Golconda or Vijayapura, we are golden because we can keep where we found the diamond our secret. The king, then, gets his precious diamond back without any war. But I don't see any way for a golden outcome to the predicament in front of us."

After dinner, as they sat around a fire, Indra Singh gave vent to deep misgivings. "What I really fear is that we might trigger a more general religious war between Hindus and Muslims. Muslims have been streaming into India for centuries now, and I know hostile feelings between us are growing. When Chandra Gupta absorbed the Muslim kingdom of Golconda into Vijayapura with Haider Ali swearing his loyalty to Chandra

Gupta, a Hindu ruler, I thought there might be a path to peace between us. If any of our plans to recover the diamond goes awry, I fear we will trigger a catastrophe that will drown the entire country in blood."

He paused again, and then spoke quietly saying, "I say we go home to Vijayapura without the diamond, and gladly offer our heads, as we promised King Chandra Gupta. The consequences are too grave. The private salvation of our family with the diamond is not worth a catastrophe that engulfs the whole world."

Around the fire, there was complete silence as each one absorbed the full meaning of Indra Singh's words. Finally, Raman Pandu replied, "Indra Singh, you speak words of wisdom and warning. Let us have a night's sleep and see if we can come up with a plan to assure us the golden outcome you seek that avoids the pathway to our personal doom."

As the men filed out from the campfire to their sleeping places, Raju lingered, staring at the fire in absolute agony. He could end all this so no one had to die. All of Indra Singh's horrors could be averted by the simple gesture of showing them the diamond. Then they could sneak back to Vijayapura: no hopeless fight at the shrine, no heads cut off in Vijayapura, and no countrywide religious war. He had the golden outcome in his *sanchi* right here.j

Briefly, his thoughts turned to Bhima's test in *The Mahabharata*: whether to fight fair, according to the warrior's code of this world, and lose—or to obey the commands of the gods to cheat and win. Raju put Bhima out of his mind. As Indra Singh, his grandfather, had just said: his family's salvation did not matter—it wasn't worth the cost of having so many people die. He would not follow the gods. Never mind that the cow Debba was still very much alive. He would break Lord Shiva's dance.

He took the diamond out of his *sanchi* and placed it by the fire at the foot of Indra Singh's chair for all to see in the morning. In the fading campfire light, the diamond radiated multi-colored beams brilliantly into the night.

CHAPTER 9

THE COW

The agony of Raju's decision was too much. Exhausted, he crumpled to the ground by the fire in a swoon. A sea of memories rolled over him in waves—remembrances of previous lives.

He remembered he was the cygnet, Babu, swimming around his mother, the beautiful white swan, Rani, in the palace Lotus Pond. He swam around and around her in circles until he suddenly dived under her, avoiding the pecks under the water from her plunging beak. When he surfaced, the first thing he always saw was the orange spot on her black beak. From this reverie, the dark day came into view: the day the king dropped his big shiny rock in the water. Babu noted the size of the rock with alarm and guessed his mother's dangerous intention.

"Don't!" he screamed. It was too late. Rani had dived after it. Babu loved his mother deeply and could not imagine life without her. He dived after her. His life went black.

The sea of his memories now focused on his mother, Kamala, who was crying. She was talking to a man who was packing his things. This must have been his father explaining the terms of his exile. Child though he was, Raju knew he now shouldered the responsibility of tending to his mother's spirits—and loving her. The curry smells of his favorite biryani dinners now wafted over the cave's fire, and Raju smiled. The smells prompted memories of Kamala's laughter at his *kabaddi* stories during these delicious meals. One night, just before the kitchen fire that swept her off the world, Kamala showed Raju her diamond necklace. "Raju, this was a gift from your father as a wedding present. I want you have it from me to pass on to your wife so that we will all be bound in a common circle of family love." Raju smiled again with the fresh memory of passing it on to Lakshmi. He sighed.

Raju was squirming and yawning awake. His thoughts turned to Debba, the cow, because he felt the warm nudge of a big nose on his forehead and the wet licks of a tongue on his cheeks. He awoke to the full face of Debba. Her big brown eyes filled Raju's field of sight. Her two eyes merged into a single brown globe that seemed to drink in the whole world. From the back of the globe, the image of Lord Shiva shimmered in his circle of fire, dancing, as it came brighter and brighter into the foreground. Soon it lit up the whole cave with shafts of fire striking the glittering lights of the diamond on the ground.

Raju gradually realized that Debba was slapping him in rebuke: "Honor Lord Shiva's instruction that Bikshu gave you," she seemed to say. With this, his resolve returned. Raju jumped up and put the diamond back in his *sanchi*. The destiny of his family was back on track. He wandered out of the cave to find a place to sleep.

Debba trailed off, swinging her tail in satisfaction.

Meanwhile, Raman was having a restless night as well. Tossing and turning, he arose from his sleeping mat under a tree. He motioned to five of his trusted troopers to join him on the hilltop above the cave. A full moon beamed upon a world of dark shadows hemmed in by lunar light that bathed the open ground in sliver. To Raman, it was a night painted by the gods. But the earthly task before him seemed to have no solution.

He summarized the dilemma to his men. "To retrieve the diamond from this *malvi* in the shrine, we've got to get past these hundred guards, snatch the diamond, and then hightail it out of the pond without anyone knowing our coming and our going—AND the commander of the guard not sounding any alarm to the soldiers on the fortress walls. So, that's what we have to do. Can any of you tell us how?"

For about an hour, at least a hundred proposals were thrown out, but none of them could guarantee the absolute secrecy required for Indra Singh's Golden Outcome. The mood of the nighttime plotters turned cranky and frustrated. Just at this moment, Indra Singh appeared. "Look, Raman, I know you and your men are trying to find my Golden Outcome, but it is beyond us. Only the gods can deliver it. And I do not see that happening on this lonely, eerie night." He paused. "Get some sleep, and tomorrow we will make

the arrangements for our return to Vijayapura—
empty-handed and then empty-headed."

No sooner had he said this than twelve dark
shadows overhead broke through a dark cloud into
the moonlight. The shadows landed and emerged
as twelve black swans, feathers glistening. One of
them stepped forward. Raman was quick to notice
the bracelet around its leg with the coat-of-arms of
Vijayapura. He jumped to his feet. "Raja, is it you?
Have you have come from Mount Meru?"

"I promised I would come when you needed
help," Raja replied. "Now that Raju has overcome
the temptation to abandon Lord Shiva's
instruction, I have been sent as a reward."

"What are you talking about?" Raman and Indra
Singh demanded in unison.

Raja shook his head and then wiggled his
beak as if he were smiling. "About Raju, that
will become clear when it becomes clear. In the
meantime, Lord Shiva sent me to bring you Indra

Singh's Golden Outcome. Here is what we must do. He pointed to the twelve sacks of divine water drawn from the River of Forgetfulness at the base of Mount Meru that each swan carried. Then he introduced the magpie, Vijaya, who was flapping his wings demanding attention. "Magpies, you see, are the only birds beside parrots that speak human speech," he explained.

Vijaya interrupted with a loud—"Caw,caw, caw. I may look like a crow, but I am bigger, and have white feathers in my wings, and I am a whole lot smarter—caw, caw, caw."

"All right, Vijaya," Raja said. "Raman, you are the only one here who understands what I am saying because of your special gift of bird speech. Vijaya will be your right-hand man—or magpie— translating your instructions to the swans, and what the swans wish to say to your troopers on the ground. You will command the operation from the hill that overlooks the shrine. Indra Singh will direct the troopers on the ground. And bring me Raju. He has a special role to play. We will launch the Golden Outcome at the next full moon."

After Raman explained Raja's plan, Indra Singh smiled. "If this plan comes from Lord Shiva himself, what could go wrong? One thing, though, I am puzzled by Lord Shiva's instruction."

Raman offered a quick solution. "Let's just ask Raju."

Indra Singh thought for a bit. "Let's not."

The month of preparations and rehearsals flew by quickly. The next full moon arrived. Everything was ready. It was time.

They all gathered on the hill overlooking the shrine. The twelve swans were there with their sacks full of the divine water from the River of Forgetfulness. Each of the water sacks, or bladders, had a tube at the bottom with a rope attached to a plug. The rope was strung around the swan's neck with a brass ring near each beak so that, on command, the swan could pull on the ring that would open the plug—and release the spray of divine waters (which were at diluted dosages to ensure their temporary effects). They were to spray the three circles of the Muslim guards around the pond. The impact would be an explosion of overwhelmingly sweet aromas from a concentrated mixture of all the flowers of India. The scent would put the Muslim pond guards to sleep. In a half an hour the scent would dissipate, and Indra Singh would deploy Raman Pandu's troopers to ensure that all the guards were asleep. Vijaya would hover over the pond guards to see if another dose were needed from a swan. Once Raman heard from Vijaya that all the guards were asleep, he would signal Indra Singh and Raju to stun the *malvi* with a dose from the divine waters and take the diamond from the case in which the scouts reported it to be. Then they would all flee from the pond and go full speed to Vijayapura with their precious cargo. This was supposed to be over in an hour. In three hours, the scent would wear off from the guards, and they would continue to man their posts, as if nothing had happened. Two swans would re-spray the *malvi* and the captain of the guard so they, too, would be none the wiser for the evening's events.

For the most part, all went like clockwork. Vijaya pinpointed the location of the guards and Raman directed Raja's swans to their targets. They started with the outer circle to ensure that none ran away. Then they switched to the second circle, which did not have enough time to react to the collapsing outer tier. The first, or inner circle, had more time to react, and started to form up. But Raman's troopers called down the last leg of the swans, whose spray quickly felled them before too much alarm had been sounded. This took all of ten minutes.

One person who had heard some of the noise from the inner line of guards was the *malvi*, who dashed back into the shrine free from the spray. He clutched the Holy *Qu'ran* and the relic box to his chest, then he froze in complete terror and absolute indecision. After fifteen minutes, he collected himself and decided to burst out of the shrine and make a run for the fortress. He opened the door to the shrine and reached with his shawl to cover his nose.

Raju saw all this from the other side of the pond. He swiftly shot an arrow that pinned the *malvi's* shawl to a post on the shrine's porch. Raju and Indra Singh then dashed across the causeway in the middle of the pond to intercept him.

"Keep your Holy *Qu'ran*, but hand over that box, and you can go on your way," whispered a breathless Indra Singh.

Tremulously, the *malvi* replied, "I see you are Hindus. What would you want with a box containing a shiny tooth of one of our most revered Muslim saints?" Forgetting himself, the *malvi* launched into a seminar explaining the moral virtues of the owner of this glistening canine tooth.

Neither of them was listening. Indra Singh was too shocked to speak, but Raju was not. Raju apologized. "We are so sorry for this intrusion, Holy One. We were mistaken. Forget we ever came here." Almost as a signal, overhead Raja sprayed the *malvi* with some of the River of Forgetfulness still left in his sack. As Indra Singh and Raju fled ahead of the spray, the *malvi* collapsed with a big smile on his face.

Unfortunately, the captain of the guard had missed a full dose of the spraying by retreating into the guard house when he heard the commotion from the inner ring of guards. He was able to sound the alarm with a weak pound on the gong before succumbing to another spraying by Raja under Vijaya's direction, who could not help ribbing Raja. "Caw, caw, caw, I told you to spray the Captain of the Guard right at the beginning, but no, you wanted to take out all one hundred guards first. But the captain is the one who can alert the fortress. Now we are cooked—caw, caw, caw."

"Well, we got him, and now we have to fly out of here, and talk about this later," Raja retorted defensively.

Up on the ramparts of the fortress, one of the soldiers thought he heard the alarm. He looked down at the shrine and everything seemed quiet. He shrugged his shoulders and returned to the game of Parcheesi he and his comrades were playing. Two hours later, getting towards morning, the sergeant-of-the-guard came by and asked how everything was going.

"It's all quiet down there," the soldier replied.

The sergeant looked down at the shrine. "Maybe it's too quiet. When your shift changes in an hour, go down and have a look."

An hour and a half later, a squad from the fortress marched to the shrine. Everyone was in place. The captain-of-the guard was at his post. The *malvi* rambled on with his tireless reading of the Holy *Qu'ran*. The fortress squad asked the captain-of-the-guard if anything had happened at the shrine during the night. The captain started to say "nothing."

Then he stopped as he noticed something white on the ground. "Wait a minute. That is a white magpie feather. What is it doing this far south? Magpies can talk, and travel with people. He must have come south with some intruders from the north." The captain ordered a detail of six archers mounted on Arabian steeds to pursue and intercept this clandestine force, or whatever-it-was, that had raided the shrine, or whatever it had done. From behind a cloud, Vijaya took all this in and flew off to give warning.

Indra Singh, Raman Pandu, Raju, Debba, and their troopers were already heading north at high speed for the Vijayapura border. But they were on foot, and the Golconda archers on horseback were gaining. Raja and his swans had brought extra bags of water from the River of Forgetfulness. Vijaya reported that the Golconda archers had split up, so Raja ordered his swans to go after the horsemen one-by-one. Eventually, Vijaya spotted four of the Golconda horsemen and Raja's swans sprayed them with the divine water. They collapsed with tell-tale smiles of bliss.

There were still two horsemen unaccounted for when the first colors of pinks, yellows, and purples melted on to the sky as it was lit by the dawn, turning the moonlight's silver ground green and brown. Indra Singh interrupted this divine painting. "It is now day, and we cannot afford to be seen in

Golconda. We will have to hide until nightfall, and then press on to Vijayapura tonight," he said.

Then he could no longer repress his worry. "If Raju followed Lord Shiva's instruction, and Lord Shiva provided us the Golden Outcome with these swans, why is the diamond still missing?"

Raju said nothing.

They waited until night. The full moon was gone, and it was a dark night. Indra Singh, Raman, and the troopers were dispirited—and not as vigilant as they should have been. As they rounded a set of boulders, the two remaining Golconda horsemen charged out on their Arab steeds, arrows flying in all directions. Raja was able to spray both horsemen with the divine water, who promptly collapsed in a heap with their horses. One of the many arrows had pierced Raja in the chest. He fell to the ground, his big wings flapping up dust all around. Indra Singh and Raman ran to the fallen swan. "Can we help you? What can we do?" they pleaded.

Raja wheezed. "There is nothing you can do. Listen carefully to me. Do not worry. The dance of Lord Shiva is being fulfilled. As I depart now to Mount Meru, I will return once more to help you finish your dance with Lord Shiva." With that, Raja expired.

While Indra Singh and Raman gathered around the Black Swan, Raju went after Debba. He found her under a tree with a Golconda arrow plunged into her heart. It was dark, and the cow appeared to be dead. Raju took a bucket of water from a nearby stream and tenderly washed her body. Since it was the dead of night, Raju had some men put the cow on a cart, and the 'Golconda raiders' marched through the night towards their forest lair in Kafiristan. At dawn, they came to a forest glen. As the rays of the morning sun caught the very placid cow, they all noticed a transformation.

Debba's face was clean and healed. Raju gingerly turned the cow's head. There it was: the orange mole under the right eye. Also, Debba was still alive. She opened her eyes just as a stupefied Raju exclaimed, "Mother!"

Somehow, the dying cow could speak—or at least Raju could hear her. "Yes, Raju, I am undergoing *samsara*, the journey from one soul to another, which is why I can talk for a little while before my next change-of-life occurs."

Raju was transfixed, but he tore himself away to fetch his father. When he found Raman Pandu, he blurted out everything at once. The only thing Raman grasped was, "Debba is about to die, but she is really Mother, and she wants to talk to you before she ascends to Mount Meru."

Not knowing what to make of this, Raman returned to Debba's side.

Debba smiled. "Raman, look at me. See the orange mole. I am your Kamala. It was the joy of my soul to have you and Raju at my side in the forest, and then to share in the Golconda adventure. Remember when we kept bumping into each other, and I licked you in the face. I was embracing you the only way I could as a cow."

A slow recognition played over Raman's face at the memories. "I can't believe it is really you, Kamala. But you know I did think about you when we were playing around.

'How could this be a cow?" I thought. "And I did feel that Raju and I were somehow linked to you. What a joy it is to know it is true and even speak to you again. I love you, Kamala, in whatever form you come."

Kamala—as Debba the cow—smiled. "I will return to this life, Raman, but in my return our marriage will be of the soul, as we ready ourselves for our final *moksha*, or release, to Lord Shiva."

She turned to Raju with a lingering look. "It is because of you, my little cygnet, that we can attain *moksha* together. Despite grave temptations, you kept your vow to Bikshu and Lord Shiva, and gained Lord Shiva's blessing for the next part of our journey."

Raju rested his head on the cow's forehead stroking his mother's orange mole. Debba's eyes closed. Kamala's next *samsara* had begun.

With Kamala's *samsara*, Raju now understood why the journey had to be undertaken in the rhythm of Lord Shiva's cosmic dance. But the only thing he said was, "Bring the cow to Kafiristan so Bikshu can come to give her a proper funeral ceremony. When we get there, I have something to tell—and something to show."

When they returned to the Forest Chamber in Kafiristan, Raju brought out his *sanchi* and tumbled it onto the big table in the banquet hall. The ebony box rolled out.

Raju opened it and handed the orange silk turban cloth to Indra Singh. "What in the world

have you been hiding there all this time, Raju?"
Indra asked.

"Open it," Raju commanded quietly. Gingerly,
the old man did. Out tumbled a glistening jewel.

"The missing Golconda Diamond," he gasped.
"How in earth did you get it?"

Raju sat them all down and related the story
of the diamond's passing from Rani the swan to
Kamala (without her ever knowing it), and to this
path of salvation via Debba the cow—all lives with
the telltale orange mole of remembrance.

With all these years of uncertainty and doubt
dissolving in front of him, Indra Singh leaped up,
and despite his advanced age, danced and shouted.
"Thanks to this revelation of Lord Shiva and to
the Three Lives of Kamala—or is it four—we
can return to the palace in Vijayapura with the
diamond—with our heads still on our shoulders!"

Shortly thereafter, Bikshu arrived from the
palace to preside over the funeral rites for Debba.

With Raman Pandu at his "wife's" side, Raju, as the son, lit the torch for the pyre. As the cow's ashes wafted towards the heavens, Bikshu issued a command to the three left behind. "As for this life, do as you are entitled to do at the court; however, remember, for the next life, you must find a particular *sannyasi* to take you all together to *moksha*. But the task of finding the *sannyasi* will fall to the woman, Lakshmi."

Overjoyed by dreams of palace life, none of them took note of these last words.

Except Raju, who was troubled by one thing. "The woman, Lakshmi, why her?"

Bikshu just smiled.

CHAPTER 10

THE PALACE

A month later, Bikshu appeared at the court of the old King Chandra Gupta during one of his *Durbars*. He approached the king and whispered in his ear. "I have some very special guests who want to see you. They are from Kafiristan."

"You mean the leader of that outlaw regime in the mountains?" inquired the king.

"The same," Bikshu replied.

"I am very eager to meet him. You have constantly put me off from all the expeditions I had planned to capture him. Now he just walks into court," the king scoffed in amazement.

Indra Singh stepped forward in front of Raju and Raman Pandu. He bowed to the king, saying: "Lord, I am the former commander of your Palace Guard, Indra Singh, reporting the accomplishment of my mission. Remember, I said you would never see me again until I had returned with the missing Golconda Diamond; if not, you could be-head me for my failure."

On cue, Raju stepped forward and handed Indra Singh his *sanchi*. Indra Singh reached in and took out the small ebony box and let the glistening diamond tumble into his hand. The entire *Durbar* gasped.

Indra Singh waited for the reality of what everyone was seeing sink in. "My Lord, here at last is your diamond," he declared. "There is no need for a war. There has been no treachery. Instead, we must rededicate our souls to the path of virtue that is reflected in this true story of the Three Lives of Kamala."

As he began the story, he handed the king the genuine Golconda Diamond. The king turned it lovingly in his hands. In his telling, Indra Singh failed to mention anything about the adventurous trip to Golconda. Sitting at her father's side during the recounting of the tale was Lakshmi, the king's daughter. She was utterly transfixed, and she stared intently at Raju while Indra Singh talked about his departure from court. When he got to the part of the story about Kamala and her devoted son, Lakshmi smiled at Raju and pointed to the necklace gleaming on her neck. Raju blushed.

For a long time, the king was simply astonished by this story, but then he gradually began to smile as a great burden on his heart began to lift. His sense of release brought on waves of happiness. He rose and embraced Indra Singh, whom he now recognized as his always faithful commander.

"Indra Singh and, of course, all of you are forgiven and reinstated. Indra, I will give you a grand estate and you will be the *maharaja* over all my *rajas*. Raman Pandu, I will make you the new commander of my Palace Guard. And you, young man, Raju, what do you want?" the king asked.

At this point, Bikshu interceded. "Your highness, there is a part for you to play in The Three Lives of Kamala as well. Her journey, after all, is not over."

"And what is that good priest?" Chandra Gupta inquired. Then he sighed. "I have no future, Venerable Bikshu. I have no heir." The king could not repress a glare in Bikshu's direction. He somehow blamed Bikshu for the birth of a daughter as a bitter joke of Lord Shiva. The father's disappointment was a heavy burden on the otherwise happy Lakshmi.

"You should be ashamed of yourself, your highness," Bikshu lectured. "When you lost

the diamond and were so utterly despondent,
I promised you an heir. At your right side is as
worthy an heir as ever lives in all of Vijayapura."

The king looked at his daughter. The surprises
on this day were too many.

Bikshu explained, "The story of Kamala, and
her quest as a woman to be a *sannyasi*, should also
confirm the virtue and capability of Lakshmi to
be a queen. Indeed, the story requires it because
Kamala still awaits her *moksha*, or release. For her
story to continue along Lord Shiva's fiery circle,
there is one more purpose that has to be fulfilled."

The king, still incredulous, asked, "And what is
that?"

Bikshu's reply shocked the king. "First, Lakshmi
must marry, and then the wheel will play itself out
to finish the cycle."

"To whom?" the king both asked and demanded.
As his eyes circled the hall, they fixed on Raju
and Lakshmi, who were obviously very intent on

joining their divergent paths from those days of schoolyard play. Grasping this slowly, the king said simply, "I see."

One person who stood riveted by this story was Haider Ali, the Muslim ruler of Golconda. Unable to contain himself any longer, he interrupted, "Before we get to this 'happily ever after,' I think there is one part to this saga that has been left out. I have just one question."

Completely taken off guard, Chandra Gupta turned to Haider Ali, in irritation, and said, "You are being rude, Haider Ali, but what is it?"

Haider Ali became dramatic. He slowly reached into the side pocket of his vest and pulled out a white feather. "So, here is my question—what is this in my hand?"

Drawn in, Chandra Gupta simply said, "A white feather."

"Yes," Haider Ali replied. "A magpie's wing feather. As everyone in this *Durbar* knows, there are no magpies in South India. However, I believe there is a particularly obnoxious one at this court."

Knowing nothing about the Golconda adventure, the king was astonished. "What is going on here?" he demanded. Indra Singh, Raman Pandu, and Raju, all three, suddenly seemed to find something fascinating about their feet. The mood of the *Durbar* turned tense. Indra Singh lifted his head and cleared his throat to speak.

Before he could utter a word, a whoosh through a window swept in an angry Vijaya. He landed on the red carpet leading to Chandra Gupta's throne. He strutted down this causeway with his stomping feet and flapping wings in a goose step cadence. As he approached the throne, he abruptly turned to Haider Ali and issued a command. "Caw, caw, caw. I will take that. Thank you very much. Caw, caw, caw." With that he flew up to Haider Ali and plucked the feather from his hand. He then made a big show of putting the feather back into his wing—and flew off. Once again, the *Durbar* was spellbound.

"Aha!" Haider Ali exclaimed. "My big mystery is solved."

"What mystery?" demanded King Chandra Gupta.

Indra Singh, Ramen Pandu, and Raju looked up. Again, Indra Singh cleared his throat. This time he spoke. "Your Highness, there was a part of the story we left out."

"What part is that?" asked the king.

"The Golconda part," answered Indra Singh.

"Aha!" Haider Ali exclaimed again.

Vijaya, in a repeat performance, whooshed down from the rafters. "Caw, caw, caw, if you say that again, I will pluck out your eyes."

"Quiet!" the king ordered. "So, what is this Golconda part?"

Indra Singh slowly related the Golconda adventure, leaving out nothing. With all the divine intervention with mammoth swans and waters of "forgetfulness," everyone was transfixed, especially King Chandra Gupta. From his original outrage, the peace of understanding and then resolution settled over him. At last, he smiled. "You have cleared up suspicions that have festered in me for years. Your long absence, Indra Singh, triggered nightmares of you plotting to overthrow me. Now I realize you just had to wait for the cow to die, and you never knew Raju had the diamond all along. Remarkable. You are a good man, Indra Singh."

"It is Raju who is the good man," reminded Indra Singh.

'Yes, I can see that," acknowledged the king. "He will make a good son-in-law and co-ruler with Lakshmi." Turning to the entire *Durbar*, he added, "When they marry, I will abdicate my throne."

At this point, Bikshu interrupted him. "Oh, king, just so you know, the pair will not be able to rule for very long because Lord Shiva has fated a special journey for them."

Chandra Gupta seemed unconcerned. "As long as they have children to secure the dynasty, I don't mind."

Raju and Lakshmi blushed but moved over to each other and held hands. Raju leaned over to Lakshmi and took the locket from around his neck. "I have this picture of the most beautiful woman in the world, but I have not been able to find her. Could it be you?"

She blushed. "I'm glad you still have it. I still have your necklace and will wear it at our wedding."

Were it not for the formal setting of the *Durbar,* they clearly would have embraced. Instead, Raju whispered, "I'll see you when I see you."

Lakshmi's smile put the whole *Durbar* in a trance. "And I'll see you when I see you."

Chandra Gupta eyed the pair and changed the subject. "Speaking of the diamond, this stone is the center of everything. From the moment you gave it to me, Haider Ali, I had suspicions about you. The gift seemed too generous, and I did not know what to make of it, even as I wore it with pride in my turban. And I harbored dark feelings towards you that grew with each year that the diamond was missing. Now I find out it was swallowed by a swan that triggered this elaborate story that has stretched across many years and lives, while I just sat here, miserable in the palace. I owe you a huge apology, my brother. May I call you brother, Haider Ali?"

In fact, Haider Ali was just as dumbfounded by Indra Singh's story as Chandra Gupta. With the mysterious attack on Golconda surely the doing of Chandra Gupta, for months he had been scheming to renew a war against Vijayapura. His mind was struggling to come to terms with Indra

Singh's confession—that he and Chandra Gupta had suspected that Haider Ali had stolen his own diamond, and now they realized that it was all a big mistake. But why did they think that, in the first place? Then he relented.

"Yes, you can call me brother."

Chandra Gupta went on. "Like Indra Singh, I have long feared a general war would break out between Hindus and Muslims. Perhaps one purpose of this story of the diamond is that Lord Shiva wants us to live in peace. To help guarantee this—Haider Ali, *Nawab* of the Muslim Sultanate of Golconda, will you serve as the Viceroy of Vijayapura? From now on, I hope to establish Vijayapura as model of a peaceful community for all of India."

Haider Ali bowed low and replied, "I am honored."

Chandra Gupta looked around the room and then declared, "One more thing—take this." Very carefully and deliberately he took the Golconda Diamond from his turban. "It is yours, Haider Ali. The Golconda Diamond should stay in Golconda."

At this, Bikshu could not restrain from making his own declaration. "With this gesture, your Highness, you give joy to Lord Shiva."

"And to my al-Allah, the one god of all Muslims," Haider Ali gratefully added.

Everyone in the *Durbar* cheered.

"Then, there is nothing left for me to do today," replied King Chandra Gupta, "but to declare this *Durbar* over, and to proclaim that the royal kitchen be open to the whole city of Vijayapura for a week of feasting."

A year later, on Raju's twentieth birthday, he and Lakshmi were married. At the ceremony, Lakshmi put on Kamala's necklace that Raju had given her. She wore it every day thereafter. Who else but Bikshu presided over the wedding, the priest who was known as "the keeper of the wheel?"

CHAPTER 11

MOKSHA

As life moved on and the cosmic wheel turned, Raju and Lakshmi had a pair of twins. As a doting grandfather and great-grandfather, Raman Pandu and Indra Singh could not keep away from the palace and its new arrivals. One day *Peda Tata* Indra Singh brought the girl, his great-granddaughter Lila, a white swan in honor of Kamala. Not to be outdone, *Tata* Raman Pandu brought the boy, his grandson Bhima, a black swan in honor of the noble bird that had saved his life at the waterfalls.

King Chandra Gupta was equally pleased and declared that the twins would be the eventual heirs to the throne and, once it was their turn, would reign as co-rulers like their parents Raju and Lakshmi. Meanwhile, Raju and Lakshmi had thrown themselves into their regal responsibilities with enthusiasm. They embarked on a road-building program throughout Vijayapura. As part of the program, they built inns and hospitals along these roads, and they had the Palace Guard train a police force to keep the roadways safe.

Still in their twenties, the pair wisely sought the advice of Bikshu. But they also reached out to Haider Ali of Golconda and Raja Mohan Singh of the Punjab. With these leaders, they worked at creating a community among their Hindu and Muslim populations. Not everything was perfect, but under the reign of Raju and Lakshmi, Vijayapura enjoyed peace and prosperity.

The years sped happily by—four, five, six, seven. Before long, Raju and Lakshmi realized the twins needed schooling, so they enrolled them in Bikshu's temple school. During this time the people in Lord Shiva's special group had become so immersed in their daily lives that they almost forgot about their common quest for *moksha* centered on Kamala and Raju.

The lone exception was Indra Singh. One morning he came to breakfast looking both exhausted—and amazed. "I had a dream last night that has to be a message from Lord Shiva," he exclaimed.

Not to have the breakfast put off, Lakshmi interrupted him. "Just eat your *idlee* rice cakes and tell us later."

Fully awake, Indra Singh shot back. "No. You must listen. This dream is a divine message for all of us."

"All right, all right," Raju broke in. "Go ahead, Grandfather."

Mollified, Indra Singh cleared his throat. "There we all were caught up in smoke from a growing fire. As we were being overwhelmed, out of nowhere whooshes in whom else but Vijaya crowing *moksha,* as a signal of our final deliverance all together."

Raju burst out laughing. "Why does Vijaya keep popping up at times like these?"

Raman Pandu said solemnly, "He must be a messenger straight from Lord Shiva."

"Anyway," Indra Singh continued. "Just after Vijaya's crowing a glorious golden chariot glided down from the clouds pulled by twelve enormous black swans the size of ostriches."

Everyone laughed. They wanted to dismiss the dream. It made them nervous. Indra Singh didn't notice as he went on. "The chariot, or sleigh really, had gold wheels and sides. There were three rows of seats with red velvet cushions. At the front of the chariot was a golden peacock statuette with its tail feathers fanned out with rubies and sapphires at their tips."

"Go on," teased Lakshmi. "You surely have an imagination."

But Raman Pandu had perked up at the mention of the swans, and asked, "What about the lead swan, Indra Singh? Was it wearing anything?"

Surprised, Indra Singh thought for a minute. "Why yes, Raman, he had a bracelet clamped onto his leg with the Vijayapura coat-of-arms on it."

Now satisfied, Raman looked at the others and declared, "The dream is real. He is my swan, Raja. At Golconda he promised to return from Mount Meru to bring us home."

A stunned silence fell on the breakfast table.

The dream provided the occasion for Bikshu, in a way, to stop the clock. He gathered the group around him at the temple—Raju, Lakshmi, Raman

Pandu, Indra Singh, and Chandra Gupta. Though he was solemn, Bikshu was smiling. "It is time to bring your group's journey to its final release of all your souls to *moksha* and their union with Lord Shiva on Mount Meru. Indra Singh and Chandra Gupta are not getting any younger, so we need to bring their release from the wheel of life before their lives end naturally, and they miss the journey with the rest of you."

"You are all bound to each other by three ties that Lord Shiva does not want to be broken. One is the saga of the Golconda Diamond. It, of course, is the symbol of earthly wealth and power— and the jealous desire for its possession is a key distraction from the beckoning of the spiritual world of Mount Meru. Raju held the diamond, and several times resisted the temptation to disobey the commandment of Lord Shiva to only reveal the diamond upon the death of Debba, the cow. Indra Singh and Raman Pandu honored pledges of loyalty to King Chandra Gupta at the peril of their lives over the supposedly missing diamond. Finally, Chandra Gupta showed the nobility of his soul by returning the diamond to Haider Ali. In this gesture, he renounced the world, and its power, in favor of the spiritual goal of *moksha*—and earned his place on this journey."

Bikshu continued. "The second tie is the reincarnated lives—the *samsara*—of Kamala, and the sign of her remembrance from life to life—the orange mole on the swan, on Kamala, and on Debba, the cow. The orange mole reminds us that though we mortals go through different lives, our souls are one, and one with Lord Shiva in his cosmic dance."

"The final tie, and the strongest one, is the sign that cannot be seen, but rings in the soul like a bell of immortality."

Lakshmi suddenly became alarmed and interrupted. "What about me? You have talked about everyone on this list but me."

Bikshu smiled at Lakshmi, and then went on, unfazed, "As I was about to say, the final tie is Raju's love. It is the tie that binds all of you on the path to *moksha*. Who is it that held this journey together through all these lives? Who is the one that kept the diamond safe for all 'the signed ones,' and who resisted practical, earthly temptations of the moment to reveal the diamond in order to honor his divine pledge to Lord Shiva, thereby preserving your group's journey to *moksha*? None other than the devoted cygnet-son, Raju. And, Lakshmi, it was Raju's love that pulled you into this circle. At the same time, through you and the twins, the line of King Chandra Gupta will continue on earth to rule in Vijayapura."

"I am sorry, Bikshu," Lakshmi apologized. "I spoke too soon."

"Not to worry, my child." Bikshu then turned to the rest of the group. "I have one more thing to say. There is one particular *sannyasi* who holds the key to your release, or *moksha*. The trouble is, this *sannyasi* is in a confused state, and needs a prod to his remembrance. As I said to you in the forest, Lakshmi, the task of finding this man, and finding a way to help him help you people, falls to you."

Lakshmi was flabbergasted. "How can I be of help? I cannot tell one *sannyasi* from another. How will I know who is the right one? I can't get one sentence out on the gods before I am utterly lost."

Bikshu was reassuring. "You were named for Lakshmi, the goddess of beauty and prosperity, traits that people see in you every day. But Lakshmi is also 'the achiever of purpose.' You may not know it, but you have a key to remembrance for the *sannyasi* that will bring him to us as the final round to your journey. Also, nuisance though he is, take Vijaya with you. He will help."

It took the group a month to absorb Bikshu's instructions for what he called "the final round." Once Lakshmi set out on her searches for the *sannyasi*, Raju insisted that she take two soldiers from the Palace Guard as an escort. She started out on her quest by visiting a different temple each day. But none of the *sannyasis* at these temples knew anything about her story. A few had heard various rumors about the missing diamond, but that was all. All the while, Vijaya kept cawing about the missing *sannyasi* not being at a temple.

Finally, at her wit's end, Lakshmi told the bird, "All right, all right, take me to where you think I can find the right *sunyasin*."

Vijaya eagerly replied, "Caw, caw, caw. Follow me if you can. Caw, caw, caw."

Lakshmi chased after the bird, while the two soldiers lumbered behind, their swords clanging in the street and occasionally tripping them up as their turbans kept unraveling. They soon fell far behind. Meanwhile, Vijaya led Lakshmi through all the twisted streets around the palace. Suddenly, they came upon a street with one vacant lot between two houses. In this space sat a *sannyasi* on a prayer mat in deep meditation. He was reciting the classic repetitive Hindu prayer or *mantra,* "Oum, Oum, Oum." This *mantra* was designed to imitate the sound of Lord Shiva's dance on the one-ness of the universe, and the devotee's prayer to feel this one-ness.

Flying over the *sannyasi,* Vijaya circled annoyingly around his head, crowing, "Caw, caw, caw, *kabaddi, kabaddi, kabaddi,* caw, caw, caw." This struck a chord in Lakshmi, even as it confused the *sannyasi.* The two took a while to grasp each other's presence. The encounter shocked them both, and it sparked a set of personal remembrances embedded in their souls.

Recovering first, Lakshmi asked the *sannyasi*, "What are you seeking, oh learned one, with your recitation?"

His reply was like a chant. "I am contemplating the one-ness of the universe, and how I can become a part of it." Then he interrupted himself, as he registered his own shock. "Where did you get that necklace?"

"From my husband. It was his mother's. I wear it every day."

"I can see that." He stared intently at the necklace. "You know, your coming here and interrupting my meditation has given me the thought that I should seek *moksha* in another way. In fact, I do not even know why I am here. This magpie compelled me to come here by constantly crowing *kabaddi* as if this was supposed to mean something, He also said this spot, where there must have been a house, is more holy to me than a temple. Who knows? Maybe it was a house of mine in a previous life and could help me in my remembrances of *samsara*. And seeing your necklace is inspiring some memory in me that tells me I should seek *moksha* with my heart, rather than with my head and all these silly *mantras*."

Not taking her eyes off the *sannyasi*, Lakshmi issued an invitation. "If you come with me, I think I can help you, and you can help me and my family."

"Really?" the *sannyasi* asked. He looked Lakshmi up and down, searching for something he recognized. Finally, he could not help himself. He got to his feet and asked Lakshmi, "Do I know you?"

"No. Not yet, oh holy one. But everything will fall into place. Come." As the *sannyasi* rose, Lakshmi took his hand.

Vijaya looked down at the pair, very pleased with himself, and flew off.

Just then, the two soldiers finally made their appearance, turbans still disheveled and swords clanging. "We are here to protect you, Your Highness."

Lakshmi could not help laughing. "If you are going to protect me, you had better get your swords fixed, and those turbans tied, so people will recognize you as the proud soldiers of the Palace Guard."

When the soldiers recovered their soldierly bearings, Lakshmi ordered, "All right soldiers of the Palace Guard, please escort me and this revered *sannyasi* to the palace."

When they arrived at the royal family's palace quarters, they opened the door to bedlam. At first glance, there was a foyer with an open-air pool in the center bordered by an array of pillars enclosing a hallway of statues of the gods. Sacrificial oil was dripping from the statues making the floor slippery. To the left was a raised landing leading into a kitchen where an untended fire was licking at a set of billowing doorway curtains dangerously close to the oil on the floor.

Indra Singh was engaged in an animated imaginary conversation with what seemed to be a ghost, while Raman Pandu was teasing him about his failing memory. To the right, Bikshu was leaving with the twins, saying he was taking them to feed the swans at the Lotus Pond. Chandra Gupta had just sat down after kissing the twins, a contented smile on his face. The sudden absence of noise from the twins broke Indra Singh from his reveries. "Where are the twins? We're supposed to be looking after them."

Raju was about to answer when he noticed that the doorway curtains had caught fire. He became alarmed. "Look out everyone. The kitchen is going to catch on fire."

Before anyone could move, Lakshmi loudly cleared her throat, "Ahem. I have brought someone for you to meet."

The *sannyasi* shuffled in, bowed low, and clasped his hands together saying the traditional greeting, "*Namaste.*"

No one responded. They stood transfixed by his eyes—actually, not quite his eyes. Staring, they all saw it.

"Mother!" Raju exclaimed.

Just then the kitchen exploded in flames. Smoke engulfed the foyer. In whooshed a triumphant Vijaya. "Caw, caw, caw. *Moksha!*

CONCLUSION: LORD SHIVA'S SMILE

Lord Shiva and Parvati were sitting on their thrones on Mount Meru. A ring of clouds blocked their view of the earth, and of the flames that were leaping skyward from the Vijayapura Palace. Suddenly, the clouds burst open as a flock of black swans pulling a gold chariot soared through.

Parvati rose from her throne clapping her hands. "My Lord, it looks like all the people in the Kamala family have arrived."

Lord Shiva sat back on his throne and took a sip of sacred water. "You know, you had a great idea using waters of forgetfulness to achieve Indra Singh's Golden Outcome in Golconda."

Parvati giggled. "Like the people on earth say, 'I am much more than a pretty face."

"Indeed, you are," Lord Shiva replied. "More than your pretty face, in her *samsara* Kamala showed herself to be a good man."

Parvati laughed again. "You mean, my Lord Shiva, Kamala the *sannyasi,* proved he was a real woman, wise as any man."

Lord Shiva smiled.

Author's Note

Timothy J. Lomperis was born and reared in India as the son of American missionaries. In his teens he paid visits to the Meenakshi Temple in the South Indian city of Madurai and fell into conversations with the temple priests. Among other things, they explained the progression of lives related in this novel. Bikshu, in the novel, is the composite of these priests.

Lomperis' fascination with Hinduism continued in graduate school in the United States. He later published the book, *The Hindu Influence on Greek Philosophy*. Most of the explanations of Hinduism in this novel are based on this study. The throne of judgment, however, in Chapter Five is taken from

Plato's "Myth of Er" in his dialogue, *The Republic*. The poem cited in Chapter Seven from the Hindu scripture, *The Bhagavad Gita*, is drawn from the 1944 translation by Swami Prabhavananda and Christopher Isherwood.

As a ten-year old boy in India, Lomperis enjoyed playing *kabaddi* with his Indian playmates, much as Raju and Lakshmi do in the novel.

Lomperis and his wife, Ana Maria, to whom this novel is dedicated, live in Maryville, Tennessee. This novel is the fruit of his efforts as a father to explain Hinduism in story form to their children (Kristina Maria and John Scott) when they were young.

Special thanks are due to Donn King of Hidden Mentor Media for bringing this manuscript to publication.

Thanks are also due to Candie Moonshower, who offered valuable editorial advice, and to

Jim Stovall for his help initiating the publication process.

Finally, the author expresses his gratitude to the many family members and friends who read revised versions of this story over the years.

177